M

Advance Praise for

AMERICAN SFUMATO

"Vojislav Pejović dissects a mind in displacement and converts it into poetry rendered in meticulously thoughtful prose. *American Sfumato* is loaded with experience, energized by writing that is beautiful, precise and generous. You'll be carrying this book around, so that you can return to it at moments of pain and joy, or read it aloud to the ones you love."

- **Aleksandar Hemon, National Book Award finalist, author of *The Lazarus Project***

"Pejović, the Balkan cousin of Kurt Vonnegut and Junot Díaz, sends his 'hyperactively pessimistic' protagonist, Miloš, tromping and romping through labs and churchyards, airy villages and suffocating apartments, disfigured beaches and misty country roads, as he looks for truth and completion in his life that was, his life that is, and his life that could have been. Along the pilgrimage, Pejović's voice lights the way, showing us that the sacred and the profane can and should exist side by side, and that we are never lost until we stop searching. This book was a cold beer in a steamy banya followed by a jump in an icy lake, leaving me spent but more alive. It was an airlock from which I was absolutely unwilling to emerge."

- **Brigid Pasulka, author of *The Sun and Other Stars***

"Dreamy and brutal, sensuous and strange, the nine-story novel that is American Sfumato looks out at the world with wide, steady eyes, taking in sex and war and the uncertain paths of the migrant without flinching. A traveler from an antique and vanished land—call it youth, call it Yugoslavia—Miloš, the protagonist of these stories, stumbles and swims toward self-knowledge through danger and wounds, only some of them self-inflicted, returning again and again in memory to a certain beach, a certain moment. In alternately piercing and deadpan prose that reveals much more of what Miloš perceives than what he thinks or understands, the painful and funny shades of his story assume a remarkable depth. 'Truth,' says Miloš, 'cannot be found by dissecting heartache, nor does it lie in folds of the flesh.' Yet where else can we seek it? In the slivered hippocampus, in the pages of this sexy, forlorn, beautiful book."

- **Joshua Corey, author of _Hannah and the Master_**

"A heady, vertiginous series of stories that invent their own chronology as they trace a life across wars and continents and love affairs."

- **Eula Biss, National Book Critics Circle Award winner, author of _On Immunity_**

AMERICAN SFUMATO

AMERICAN SFUMATO

— a novel in nine stories —

VOJISLAV PEJOVIĆ

TORTOISE BOOKS

CHICAGO, IL

FIRST EDITION, OCTOBER, 2019

©2019 Vojislav Pejović

Published in the United States by Tortoise Books

www.tortoisebooks.com

ASIN: XXX
ISBN-10: 1-948954-08-7
ISBN-13: 978-1-948954-08-2

This book is a work of fiction. All characters, scenes and situations are either products of the author's imagination or are used fictitiously. Any resemblance to actual events or locales or persons, living or dead, is coincidental.

Cover image by Aleksandar Đuravčević

Cover design by Aleksandar Đuravčević, Vojislav Pejović, and Ysabel Pinyol

Tortoise Books Logo Copyright ©2019 by Tortoise Books. Original artwork by Rachele O'Hare.

TABLE OF CONTENTS

Then take me disappearin'
Through the smoke rings of my mind
Down the foggy ruins of time
Far past the frozen leaves
The haunted frightened trees
Out to the windy beach
Far from the twisted reach
Of crazy sorrow

Words by R. A. Zimmerman, a.k.a. Bob Dylan, allegedly heard by Miloš, the protagonist of these stories, one cold evening in an overheated car, while driving by the frozen Lake Michigan.

That what happened
Closely resembles a miscarriage
Where between coitus and birth
The boundaries of time have been swept away
And everything occurs
Impossibly simultaneously

Danilo Kiš, Golden Rain [fragment], translated by Miloš.

NIGHT SWIM

(for Ruth Blatt)

We've barely made it up the mountain when Father's litany begins: the snow, the slippery road, our Yugo's balding tires. Snow in April, passes through my mind—just like thirty-something years ago. That summer, for the first time, they took me to the house: my misshapen head in my mother's cleavage, my baby folds taunting the mosquitoes. I imagine Father, taking forever to assume the position and finally snap the photo; there's V, too, waiting impatiently and then lunging forward, determined to lift a thick apostrophe of hair off my mother's face (her hand retreating in a spectral blur). The mosaic shade of *zelenika* trees stirs up the milk of our skin, creating a contrast almost audible: like a subdued call of the cicadas, or maybe tires running over gravel. And the driver in front of us veers off the road: Father's knuckles turn pale at the steering wheel, his mouth fills with spit-speckled curses—one for the driver, one for the snow, one for the fucking life that won't leave you alone.

Tell me again about Dolly the sheep, he insists, and I try once more to explain the principles of reproductive cloning. Why didn't you become a lawyer, he then asks; that way, you wouldn't have left. I say nothing in response. We turn downhill, and the view of the lead-colored sea gives way to a barren landscape of mountains, overgrown with patches of shrub. I remember legends V used to tell: about the air raids, the caves, the plans to press him to her chest, jump into a ravine, and kill them both. There she is, in front of us, in her faux-mahogany confinement, braving the precipices one last time. Chances are, her last driver will make it to the city: the snow is abating, we can tell he's handling the curves much better.

The next day, an icy wind rattling our resolve, we spend six hours in a doorless chapel and one more huddled around the gravesite. Every now and then Father disappears, returning calmer and redder in the face. The broken voice of V's oldest relative cracks together with the only functioning loudspeaker; soon thereafter, everything is over. It is unseasonably cold, passes through my mind, as earth starts bobbing on the coffin, and as Father grabs me by the shoulder, scared that he might fall in.

I decide to stay another week, maybe even two. Father needs me, and the cold spell was, after all, just an aberration: the green shots of spring are everywhere, together with the grains of pollen and the miniskirts. Our place—funny I should call it that—reeks of neglect and nausea. With me around, Father retreats to the role of the diseased (the disease being a hybrid of self-loathing and addiction), which means that I call all the shots and buy all the groceries. I keep the windows permanently open, the door to the balcony constantly ajar. Father zooms in and out of the apartment, irritated by the chill, confused by all the fresh air. He screams at me for hiring the painters; I scream at him that some of Mother's paintings are missing. Let's go to the house for a few days, I say, aiming at reconciliation. He just shakes his head wildly, asks that I reveal where his supplies are, then adds: only if you're crazy. It's not the same place anymore, I told you a million times.

Some of my old friends take me out, and I end up hooking up with T. She's new in town, in the sense that she arrived after I had left. A refugee, I ask, but then backtrack, apologize, overcompensate by offering a whole-body massage. Aren't you, too, she replies, which only makes things worse—the only danger I was escaping was myself. We go out a couple of nights, sometimes hand in hand. I notice that the city has changed, pretty much the way I saw it on the Internet and heard over the phone: it is a shinier, louder, almost happier place. T has learned to love it, wishes I could stay longer. The paint job is done; Father barricades himself in his room (the one that used to be theirs), closes the windows, rolls down the shades. Except for that fortress of misery, the apartment appears almost new: at least ten years of solitude have been erased, the rectangular ghosts of Mother's works included (three oil canvases, one aquarelle). Through the locked door, Father yells that he preferred it the way it used to be.

I stop by the cemetery. The heaps of flowers over V's grave are in full, spectacular decay. The slab of concrete at Mother's is devoid of any vegetation, except for a few shy patterns of lichen at the corners. I stay with Mother for a while, a meter or so above the spot where, I imagine, the remains of her left shoulder must be. Later that evening, I ask for the keys to the house, disregard Father's protestations, and send an email to the lab, informing them that my family affair will require at least a few more weeks. The following morning T and I are in her car: up the mountains, down to the seaside.

T finds the view of the bay breathtaking, no matter how many times she sees it; truth be told, so do I. We stop in Kotor to visit my aunt, only to find out that Father was right, that dementia has been gnawing at her mind. She doesn't recall that she had a sister, or that the sister had me. Luckily, she still knows her own daughter, maybe even picks up on her caregiver resentment. I used to divide my summers between the house and my aunt's, I explain, then feel guilty again: I obviously have a surplus of stay-in quarters, whereas T had to leave hers at gunpoint. My cousin makes us a delicious calamari salad; we even manage to laugh at the table, reminiscing over our childhood years. She objects at first, but ultimately accepts the money I brought. I insist that she come to Chicago someday, then remember that Alzheimer's can take up to ten years to completely suffocate one's brain. We exchange hugs and good-byes. I know you, the aunt suddenly exclaims: you're the boyfriend of that Asian girl.

Before leaving Kotor, we buy a few days' worth of groceries. I ask that we also stop at the nursing home, where Father and I picked up V's body a mere week and a half ago. In the meantime, the honeysuckle on the wrought-iron fence has started to bloom; the first bees are levitating dutifully. A few residents notice our presence and start approaching the gate, slowly, unsure whether someone has come to tuck them in or take them away. We run back to the car, for the first time feeling guilty simultaneously. After a few kilometers of asphalt and a few more of gravel, we park in front of the house.

T and I make the place inhabitable in only an hour. The table, the chairs, and the bench are on the patio; the windows are wide open; even the bed linens are stretched out in the breeze, in an attempt to tame the thick, intoxicating swirl of lavender aromas. (Which are impossible to get rid of completely: there is a large bush, right by the patio, full of miniscule violet bulbs.) It's been ten years since my last visit. V was still in good shape, most of her neighbors were alive. Now, the village appears completely deserted—the house façades, with their blinds and doors shut, resemble death masks chiseled in white stone. The only sounds are those of insects and the sea. (One can also make out a mechanical purr, most likely from the roadwork we saw on the way.) I take T by the hand and into the bedroom. We make love by an open window, screaming for the sake of it.

The night falls and we prepare dinner—mushroom omelette with aged pecorino that my cousin gave us—outside, on a butane-powered cooker I've known all my life. Father did inform me that there's power now, tap water even, but I guess I didn't want to know anything about it. We take out a cot and blow out the gas lamp, eavesdropping on the crushing waves, looking up the crowns of *zelenika* trees. It doesn't take much effort to summon V's skinny apparition (her hair undone, gas lamp in her hand), pleading voicelessly that we go inside. I wake up in the middle of the night, shivering, shaking T's shoulders, asking if she also heard someone's voices. Or were those just cries from V's many stories still roaming the house, lost without their departed conjuress?

The next morning clouds gather in an instant, unleashing a heavy, chilling shower. We decide to stay in, cook, and have lots of sex. In the intermissions, I take notice of Father's silent presence. First, the lavender: all those handfuls of twigs we found in the closet looked recent, suggesting that he had been here a week or two before the news of V's impending death sent me rushing home. Second, newspapers from a few months ago had been used to defrost the fridge. Third, the very act of defrosting points to someone having been here for at least a couple of weeks and needing the fridge in the first place. Needless to say, it couldn't have been V, considering what had happened, and the fact that she spent the last six months in that nursing home, unable to do much more than moan endlessly. (Moan endlessly: that's what the head nurse told me, as we were lifting the lid off the coffin so I could identify the body, tranquil and shriveled. Father waited outside, fainthearted as ever.) Finally, I find one of Mother's missing paintings, the aquarelle, deep in the drawers. Did Father want to redecorate the place? And if so, where are the three oils? Or did he intend to move in once V passed away, occasionally getting wasted on the beach? Or was the lavender a son's belated act of kindness, in case she miraculously recovered and came home?

We both wake up from a dream that featured some heavy machinery: in T's case, it was a Yugoslav People's Army tank, stuck in the dark Pannonian mud, burping up Coke bottles instead of shell cases;

I dreamed of an aquaplane that couldn't take off, ropes of seaweed wrapped tight around its pontoons. In our separate sleeps, we both also heard human voices, and felt that those may have come from outside our dizzied heads. This was strange, indeed: just like the night before, all the windows in sight were dark when we went to bed. For all we know, we are the only people in the village.

Apparently, another rainy day is upon us; we're rapidly depleting our food reserves, but getting better and better at fucking. After a feast of pan-toasted bread and canned tuna (an experience significantly enhanced by a flood of olive oil and a storm of freshly ground pepper), we decide to accept Father's gift of electricity, turn on the radio, and make sure that no major catastrophe has befallen the world (the minor ones—say, a retired warrior on a killing spree—being barely newsworthy). We learn with relief that a strip of sunny days is about to unfold.

You're going to love this, I say, pulling at T's hand, taking her over the rocks and through a labyrinth of bushes. Father claims that, a long time ago, before there was tap water and asphalt road, the beach we're about to step on was the only pristine cove on the Adriatic coast. No more than a few strokes into the water—I go on—the seaweed gets so dark and thick, you'd think it's been planted there on purpose, to chase away visitors, to cover up something sinister and unfathomably vile. That's why I mostly swam at night: when the water was uniformly dark, and it was warmer to be in than out. T smiles, content to see my best boyish self. I smile, too: half with the thrill of reuniting with the only place I was ever close to calling sacred, half scared that there will be visitors polluting my innocence with their sunscreen and their food leftovers. (Half forgetting, of course, that that had happened before: last time when I tried to get there with Kumiko, but that's another story.)

Suddenly, as if stepping through a massive, rustling curtain, the vegetation vanishes. We raise our palms to our eyes, assaulted by the sun and the whiteness of the pebbles. Our pupils shrinking, we realize that the beach is sliced up with concrete walkways, all converging—in a few zigzagging segments—on a dock that has taken up a good half of the waterfront. At first, stunned by the change, I stand motionless, unable to think, but then swift and mighty hindsight provides me with the following: observed from above, the beach must look like a rock where an oversized sea monster decided to rest, unsure whether to dive in or crawl ashore. On each walkway, at intervals measuring a dozen or so of my hurried steps (yes, I'm moving now, anxiously), handfuls of corroded rods are sprouting on each side, like (a) hairs on a rust-haired spider, (b) iron stamens waiting for their pollinator (Who could that be? What fruit could be borne out of that act?), or (c) something even more creepy and disgusting, for which there is no easy simile. The monster, already somewhat polished by the elements (suggesting at least three to four years of abominable and inglorious existence), glistens eerily atop the pebbles' muted sheen, making the occasional clusters of goat droppings on its surface that more visible. T looks at me bemused, wordlessly asking if that indeed is the place I vexed so adolescently about, and then, her shoes in her hand, steps on one of the zigzagging limbs, determined to teach me the advantages of confronting life's spiders. Her arrival at the monster's demibody is greeted by gurgling in its underbelly, by foaming at its feeding hole.

My pace faster and faster, I examine that bizarre deformity from all sides. There is no one in sight, but whoever did this will return: no one builds an ugly arachnoid maze on once-unspoiled beach and then fails to show up; no one erects a seaside shack (a huge open bar in front of it), names it, of all names, O Paraíso, and disappears forever. Furious, foolish, I knock wildly on heaven's door. (The joke is T's, I'm too upset for humor.) The plank that bolts the door carries an inscription that reads I. Montenegro; is that someone's name, or some shack-building company's idiotic logo? T proposes that we stay: after all, we obviously are alone and can proceed with our plan to swim and have fun naked (an entire half of the beach—she jokes again—being in excellent condition). Eventually I agree, but not before releasing a long, rebellious stream of urine into the water, standing proudly on the edge of the concrete fucking marina.

In the early afternoon we drive back to Kotor, in need of fresh groceries, an espresso bar, and a decent cellphone signal. Should we go to the police, I ask, but T just gives me a look that signals incredulity and gentle pity, then returns to her conversations (parents; the law office where she works; someone else, who remains a mystery). Although this was supposed to be a carnal folly and—I was explicit, yet gentle—nothing more, I notice that I've become accustomed to her presence. How much longer can I, can either of us, take it? Is there any way I could fit her in my life *over there*? I think of looking for an internet café and checking my work email, but decide that I can still hide behind my grief. I do call Father, several times, only to endure his not picking up. Worried, I call our neighbors. They did see him today, and last night, too. I hope he'll make it through a few more days without drinking himself into madness.

T is gone procuring food, while I try to find the best spot for a coffee. After a few rounds through the old town maze (my internal map of the narrow passageways still largely intact), I settle for a group of comfortable rattan armchairs, hidden behind a wall of reed scaffolding and creepers. In spite of a sense of privacy—a necessary ingredient of all peace and luxury—and an exquisite, richly foamed cappuccino, unsettling thoughts keep circling through my head, like buzzards looking for the decaying leftovers of joy. What if I knew the people who desecrated my own private paradise? What if their act was illegal indeed? And where have the villagers gone, all old and frail? Why did Father never tell me anything about it? Luckily, the café's loudspeakers go ablaze with some obnoxious Balkan fare (brass band, wild percussions, sad song about copulation and intoxication), dispersing the thoughts, almost forcing me to focus on the freshness of the air, the brightness of the sky.

The people are happy: everyone in town seems to be outside, eager to bask in the late spring sun, unconcerned with phantom beach wreckers and their abominable deeds. Inspired, I ask T whether she'd be into some spectacular seafood, confident that I'll find a particular restaurant I've only heard about; being (having been) a local, I should know where it is. T, as it turns out, has been there many times—doesn't say with whom. The only person I'm capable of surprising is me.

The cod salad, the octopus salad, the sardines; the wine, grilled squid, mussels à la Marinière: T's eyes are wide open yet calm, glistening with profound satisfaction for the first time since we've met. I lick my fingers, covered with the olive oil, rosemary needles, salt, then offer to do the same with hers. A small beach, property of the restaurant owner, stretches a few meters away from our table; we take a dip, release some unintelligible sounds of pleasure and fullness. Did she enjoy it this much with my friends, I ask myself, then start pondering the meaning of that question. To clear my mind, I decide to make a few quick turns in the water, taking in the landscape of the mountains with my spin: their barren slopes rushing to the sea, their imprint in my brain quivering and blurry.

We drive back to the house, light up a few candles, open a bag of freshly baked pastry. I notice for the first time that the tree crowns by the patio form a perfect frame for the sun's distorted orange, cut in half by the horizon line. I wonder whether such a conspiracy of branches is just nature's accident, or another hint at Father's village adventures. I remember well our summers together: his passion for sunsets; the obsessive evening strolls he and Mother used to take; my staying with V, massaging her back, absorbing the never-fading luminescence of her nightmares.

I must have been silent for a while, because the sun is gone by the time T asks why exactly did I have to leave. I told you, to become a neuroscientist, I say, but by now she full well knows that that answer is incomplete. There was a girl, too, I add; I thought I should follow her but never saw her again. No one I know is as full of shit as you are, she says, baring her teeth more than usual, looking fierce, more attractive than ever. Her thinly veiled, unexplained anger feels almost deserved; I can see it swelling up, hope for more of it. The first uncomfortable silence between us is short, however, without a chance of brewing into a fight and a session of make-up sex: the deep purr of an engine and the voices, real ones, can be heard again. We conclude that there must be a boat parked in our marina, hosting a group of happy, insufferable people.

The next morning we hurry to the beach and discover Jeff, a deeply tanned, middle-aged, beer-bellied man, sprawled across a recliner in front of the shack, wearing nothing but a tight, striped swimsuit and a captain's hat. The open bar is fully stocked now, its hanging bottles shining auburn and ultramarine in the morning sun. Jeff invites us to join him at a table. In spite of his name, his Serbo-Croatian is perfect, albeit with a thick, undeterminable accent. We learn that *the complex* belongs to a foreigner, the generous Mr. Montenegro, well-connected and influential, but above all a really, really nice fellow, someone whose folks were from around here and who was eager to invest in his grandparents' old country, torn by a silly war and grand misfortune. What's his real name, I demand (and why his obsession with ugliness, spiders?), but the question remains unanswered, not least because a red-haired, freckled, green-eyed girl emerges from underneath the bar, dressed in an extra-skimpy polka-dot bikini. Her face is pretty, but with black and purple bruises underneath both eyes. She steps forward smiling, without haste, carrying her perfect body with confidence of a tightrope artist. She asks, dreamily, about our drinks, mentions casually that everything is on the house, disregards the fact that both of her areolae, earth-brown and rough, are protruding from their tiny covers. Jeff nods in approval, as if he himself had taught her that strange choreography of servitude and lust. T shuffles in her seat; I can sense her mounting discomfort, feel almost grateful for it. You can call me Dana, the girl says; I take care of the place when the boss isn't around. She goes back to the bar and bends over to reach for our drinks, leaving us to stare at her perfect rump. Taking in her every move, Jeff mentions that the boat—a yacht, really, and a real beauty: when you see it, you'll want to fuck it—is his main responsibility. (*And*, he adds with a whisper, *keeping an eye on her*.) Dana returns to the table, holding four sweaty bottles by their necks. Before handing them to us, she rubs their bottoms against her tight abdomen and releases a suppressed groan, faking a beer-commercial orgasm. Jeff applauds, happy as a child, as she takes a bow with a short, throaty laugh. I smile politely, grin to signal gratitude, take my bottle and bring it to my mouth. Suddenly, a wave of merciless scents permeates my mind: the sea in which she swam, the sunscreen, her mildly fermented sweat. One tiny leap of fancy and I'm tasting her meaty lips; her dark, rotund nipples; the warm grains of salt on her neck.

Back in the house, T insists that we leave right away, immediately, now. I protest, claim that that would be a bad idea: we're invited to the yacht, the mysterious boss is going to be there. I need to look that person in the eye and ask him a question or two: Who gave him the permission to build a marina? Where are all the villagers? What happened to Dana's face? Is she a minor? Do her parents know that she's manning a seaside bar, together with some casting reject from a child molestation movie? We argue for about an hour. She finally agrees that we stay, provided that I (a) don't get drunk, (b) never leave her side, and (c) take us out of there at the first sight of anything weird. Truly and honestly, I say, I just want to get to the bottom of this: V is dead, the beach has been ruined; I don't belong here anymore. In a show of seriousness, I make her a nice butane-powered dinner (white wine saltimbocca, a few improvised crepes) and pack the few belongings we've brought with us. I also take Mother's aquarelle (man, woman, and child in a snowball fight; everything a smear of white, gray, or blue, except for their deep-red faces), wrap it in a pillowcase, and lay it, carefully, in between my T-shirts and underwear. After that, hand in hand, we observe another sunset Father would approve of.

Nancy the Beautiful is anchored in its full nouveau-riche glory: its stupid name in gold and cursive, its cabin windows dark, its two decks infested with color bulbs and people who produce a joyous chatter. On the walkways, each cluster of iron stamens hoists an ignited torch, as if rust took its oxidized nature to the extreme and flourished into fire. No one seems to notice that we're there, alone on one of the fractured paths, halfway between the vegetation and water. As we take in the scene and exchange worried glances, and as T utters, speaking for us both, that the best would be to go home this instant, Dana coalesces out of thin, fragrant air, wraps her arms around our waists, and pushes us toward the bar. Her fingertips, resting on my hip, give me an instant erection. You're going nowhere, guys, at least not till we've had a few drinks together, she says; everyone else on this fucking beach is way too old for me. She is barefoot and wears a tight green dress that shows no lines of underwear; she smells like summer rain, like vapors rising from the freshly plowed earth. I can tell that T, too, has an urge to grab her by the tits and slide her tongue down her killer body.

Both blushing, we follow Dana to the bar, order something non-alcoholic. Our hostess pretends not to notice our confusion, starts talking about the many trips they took together: Sicily, Malta, Côte d'Azur; they're planning Brazil, too. Who are they, I ask, proud that I'm regaining bits of self-control. The boss and Jeff and I, of course, she answers matter-of-factly; everyone else is just a guest. Them too, I ask, pointing at a couple of bodyguard types, the only people around who do not drink or engage in some cackle of a conversation. Privilege demands protection, doesn't it, she says, playing with a lock of her dirt-red hair. Only then do I notice the makeup on her face, the fact that her bruises are just barely visible. Do you know what happened to the people who lived here, I blurt, instantly regretting that I revealed my game so early. Dana stops smiling, asks what I meant by that. Why are all the houses empty, I say, trying to sound as neutral as possible. She smiles again, says I'll tell you all about it when I'm back, takes a quick turn, and disappears into the crowd. T grabs me by the hand, repeating let's go, let's go already. I ignore her and squint really hard, scanning the faces, looking for someone I might recognize: from the city, Kotor even, anyone who could help us should the need arise. No luck: all those chatty people are like one semiconscious, bubbly organism, feeding on martinis, vodka, and the goodwill of some faceless foreigner with a fake name. There is something happening, though: a window on the lower deck is open, with two silhouettes—Dana and the boss, I'm sure—staring back at me. As they break apart to turn off the light, I catch a glimpse of the cabin's walls.

The plan comes to me quickly. I take T into darkness, away from *O Paraíso*, hoping that we'll attract no attention, mere lovebirds looking for a mating spot. We follow the water and soon reach the bushes; no one seems to be on our trail. T should hide and look out for danger. At the first sign of anything suspicious, or if I'm not back within twenty minutes, she should run straight to the car and drive back to the city. Yes, I know what I promised, and no, there is no way I could change my mind.

All those bodies I bump against feel almost artificial, absorbing the force of my hurried steps, not turning once to see who made them spill their champagne and their curaçaos. With a corner of my eye, I spot Dana's head, bobbing in agreement in front of some featureless party people. One tiny flight of stairs and I reach the cabin, *I. Montenegro* engraved on its door. It is locked, but not well enough for the impact of my heel. I work in the light that seeps in from the outside and find quickly what I'm looking for—a maritime version of our living room wall. Even the order of the paintings has been preserved: on the left and right, the same heart-shaped silhouette of a woman and a man, his head resting in her lap. In the darkness, my mind supplies the details: in the left painting, a cage of elongated shadows, imprisoning the couple in their amorous repose; on the right, a dark magenta sun, afloat between their torsos, as if foretelling something big and momentous—on their minds (a son) and in her abdomen (a son; intestinal cancer). In the central painting, a woman holds a baby: his head in her cleavage, his fat folds taunting the mosquitoes, their features shrouded by shadows that corrupt them like a memory. In a drawer, I find a dry towel. I take down the paintings and wrap them in a bundle.

That, I believe, is ours, says Dana.

I turn around and see her at the entrance, paired with the same silhouette I saw before. You can't escape, says a man's raspy voice. Someone flips the switch. I lunge forward, slap Dana across her face, shove the man aside. On my way up the stairs and onto the deck, I get a sense that I've seen him before: his red hair, his face riddled with acne.

I hear whistles, see the bodyguards storming the deck, feel the confused commotion of the guests— some throwing themselves overboard, giggling mindlessly, their glasses in their hands. I try to find an exit, but everything is turmoil: muscular men charging, elbowing the befuddled guests; two fiery heads screaming commands, one bleeding from her nose; lines with color bulbs shaking wildly; a hand that grabs my throat. I've got him, I've got him, Jeff squeals in triumph, as his fingernails sink into my skin and as I start losing consciousness. With my last strength, I lodge fingers into his eyeballs, kick him in the crotch, and push him toward the first advancing guard. I press the paintings to my chest and jump into the water.

As I plunge into darkness, the first sensation is cold. The second is pain: another body hits the water, something hard gets me in the head. I lose my bundle, hear a loud click; half a dozen underwater lamps awaken at once and transfix the scene with their kilowatt beams. The towel unfolds and releases the paintings. Everything floats up. My eyes, burning with sea water, move to take in the thick carpet of seaweed: dark green, dense, in synchronous motion. I, too, rise to the surface, where I'm welcomed immediately with blows to my head.

I wake up on the beach: my head in T's lap, my whole body aching. I can inhale only through my mouth, my rib cage expanding in pain. The yacht and the people have vanished; the sky is deep blue, punctuated with rare fading stars. Above us, a strange, shape-shifting cloud is turning darker with each twist, as if mopping up the night. I'm sorry, I'm sorry for everything, I sputter, but T doesn't say a word. In silence that needs no interpretation, she lifts me up and helps me through the shrub. As we walk, my ears start humming with a sound that almost makes sense, which I soon decode as my own unstable heartbeat. After half an hour of my moaning and grunting, we get to the house, the rancid smoke rising from its windows. The remaining flames are jittery and timid, like ghosts who've lost their way between the worlds. Father is there, too, his eyes bloodshot, his face and hair ashen. T shakes me off and I let her drive away, without as much as calling her name.

I curl up on the back seat of our Yugo, staring at the smoldering roof beams. Father starts the engine, unleashes a monologue of curses and cries: he hates me for being so arrogant and stupid; for not listening to his pleas and warnings; for not thinking twice why V took all those pills; for trying to reverse the wheel of fucking history; for ruining his attempt to save the fucking house; for not giving that red-haired asshole what he wanted. Go fuck your Dolly the sheep, he goes on, swigging mightily from some unlabeled bottle. Go fuck yourself, you prissy smartass asshole; go clone yourself in a lab and never come back again. My head is buzzing with his rage, with our Yugo's erratic vibrations. I take in the first morning of my new life: the smell of our seat covers, the trembling tops of palm trees, the vertiginous mountain we've started to climb.

TABLEAU OF DISCONTENTS

Nuages

The rare moments of clarity, like the one when I sank down on the pavement across from the downtown gas station, shortly before midnight in August nineteen-ninety, do not need a soundtrack. Solitude is much more important, or at least being with no more than one other person. It may also help that the asphalt and concrete exude the daily heat, that the hill nearby is besieged by cicadas, that the station's balding attendant—straddling a back-broken chair, his wet shirt spliced with his hairy chest—is listening to an undistinguishable radio program. He must realize that I'm there, that he's being watched, but his face is immobile, oscillating between dead and alive, which no doubt is an artifact of erratic illumination: dirty green-yellow letters (JUGOPETROL) are turning on and off haphazardly, multiplying their impermanence in the oily puddles. Despite the tang of petrol derivatives (*seaside, oh, seaside,* howls a pack of Prof. Pavlov's dogs inside my head), the hot air smells mostly of the evergreen forest that shrouds the hill. Those essences, inhaled through the filters of late night and late adolescence, make the station assume the features of a beach concealed by a labyrinth of shrub, an exact double of the one that, according to Father's reliable testimony, once was the most pristine cove on the Adriatic coast.

The beach vanishes, and so does the attendant. The speakers crack louder and the first few bars—solo vibraphone—fill up all visible space; the small square surrounding the station is encapsulated now in a membrane of honey. (Clarity and mild hallucinations are not mutually exclusive.) The meandering melody, carried by the metallic ting, is taken over by a guitar and a bass, and then handed back to a bony black guy with a long mallet in each hand. (Milt Jackson, Joe Pass, Ray Brown: I'll find that out not long afterward.) With the last solo fading out, the membrane of honey evaporates into the vast bin of darkness. Whoever I'm waiting for must have arrived—the rest of the night remains submerged in the certainty of oblivion.

The Wall

I keep up with them, although there's still time to get away and go home. A shredded male voice roars on about drinking the blood of infidels; the white-hot throats echo the refrain, emphasizing every syllable. Someone from the crowd shoots in the air, once, twice, and the long banners go wild, like eels in a net. The howling from the throats swells up, pressing on my eardrums. The crowd moves past an abandoned gas station and halts underneath a churchyard, at the foot of a hill sprouting black cypresses. I remember the church, I went there as a child: once with V, because I was curious and insisted, and once alone, to prove to myself that I wasn't scared. Above us, a bearded metropolitan with immobile eyes (I remember them from TV) stands as if straddling something underneath his robes. To his right is a red-headed man also clad in black, with a face strange and tortured, as if riddled with acne. To their left is a platoon of young men in camouflage attire, who first cross themselves and then fire a few bursts of lightning rounds into the night sky. The howling becomes unbearable. My head is spinning, but I don't know whether due to a sudden dizzy spell (What's wrong with me?) or because I realize that I'm practically weightless, supported from all sides by excited human flesh. The metropolitan raises his arms and the song of bloodthirst is cut mid-syllable. The shots die down, the eel banners limp down their staffs. *May God help you!* he shouts, his lips grazing the microphone membrane. *Christ is born!* he goes on (roaring, banners, shots); *Let's purge the pest from our flock!* (Roaring, banners, shots, songs.) The congealed crowd boils over; the erratic streaming of the bodies takes me to the wall that supports the churchyard plateau. I recognize my chance, reach for the wall with both hands, fight my way toward it, follow it like a blind man. Soon I'm all alone, filtered through a row of cypresses into a space no one else seems willing to invade. I realize why, because my innards are suddenly awake with fear that lay dormant for years: the abandoned cemetery is right in front of me, many tombs are gaping open. The hum I left behind sounds more and more like a distant storm, but one of those that could unload at any moment. I clench my teeth, chose the company of the dead. To suppress the growing sense of horror (and, I'm ashamed to admit, a sudden urge to empty my intestines), I start thinking about Father, whether he'll be home when I return. Struck by another dizzy spell (What's going on? What's going on with me?) I sit down on the closest tomb. With the remaining strength, I move my feet to check whether there's a missing slab of stone on the sides, a passage for rats and apparitions. I then rest, curled like a rain worm, on the cracked surface. I read someone's eroded name with my fingers.

Halftime

The flakes are coming down in droves, in vertiginous trajectories and with great persistence, as if laden with the knowledge that the snow doesn't stay here long. I read recently how Colonel Aureliano Buendía, faced with a firing squad, recalled the moment his father took him to see ice for the first time. On the verge of adolescence, I find all that laden with symbolism, replete with hints of synchronicity. Then there's Mother, emerging from the whirlwind, and an amorphous lump of snow that flies up from her palms and lands on my face. Soggy, defeated, I have no choice but to laugh. Through the clogged ears I hear the impact of a real snowball, hard-pressed and well defined, a clear *SLAM!* against her winter coat, and then Father's: *One-zero! One-zero for me!* We keep chasing each other across the squeaky parking lot in front of an abominable high rise and then stumble up the stairs, five stories high, hungry and exhausted. Mother is content, all faint smiles as she sets down the *džezva* pot on the stove, content while feeding the laundry machine with our socks and underwear. Father's content, too: the TV is on, the game has begun, and his muscles, still tense from an unplanned effort, make him feel like a soccer player, one of those on the screen, clad in tight black leggings and in full pursuit of a bright-red ball across a snowy pitch. (On the screen, the ball resembles a crimson snowflake.) Before the first half is over, Mother and Father are done with their coffee and cigarettes. The sky is the color of asphalt; it's coming down stronger than ever. Luckily, the snow doesn't stay here long.

Beneath the Skin

What am I doing here? Despite the winter, days in the city are long and unbearable, nights after rainy afternoons particularly so. Under different circumstances, I would have sailed away to days that'll come and worlds that are no longer. Here and now, however, I can't ignore the prickly itching on my face, which renders useless my attempts to disappear. I was reading about it recently, although the source did not inspire confidence: burdened by a deep, unsatisfied need, women sometimes change their hair. I first cut down my beard with Mother's old scissors and then shaved the rest using Father's razor of questionable sharpness. Other than the itching, however, I feel no particular change. I had to leave the apartment, it was for the benefit of us both. I'm pacing down the deserted promenade, past the abandoned gas station at the foot of a hill, and make a turn toward the park that houses a military compound. As my beard was growing—it took weeks, if not months—strange things were happening: people were becoming firearms owners; musical trends were escaping the constraints of taste (any taste); there were a couple of genuine massacres across the border. (The border's new, too.) Last but not least—actually, the worst of all—I still have no clue where Kumiko has gone. Most likely, I will never know. Most likely, I will never know. I like the rhythm of those syllables: the sequence creates an impression of completion, although the desired outcome—finding out where the hell Kumiko disappeared to—could theoretically take forever. I also like the quasi-nonchalance with which I, all of a sudden, treat the object of my obsession. Who knows, maybe the urge to remove all that facial hair did originate somewhere deep inside. To my great surprise, the second contemplation of an essential, unsatisfied need in just one evening leaves me completely undisturbed. Instead, the disturbance comes from outside, jerking me brutally out of the first stream of consciousness in at least six months that actually felt good, that didn't make my temples pulse with pain or threaten to turn into a vortex of insomnia and sweet fantasies of my own funeral. The music from somewhere nearby—did I mention the declining trends already?—is wrecking my nerves, especially like this, when it's muffled and subdued. It seems that the monotonous crescendo is due to the Doppler effect: the ever louder booming indicates that the music's source (a car, I can see it) is approaching. I'm walking by an enormous puddle, but luckily, the car is driving in the opposite lane. Or it was: the vehicle changes lanes in an instant, plunges into the puddle at full speed and with full deliberation, and a wave of icy, filthy water covers me from head to toes. I imagine their screams of delight; I wish to find out who they are, to murder them one by one in their sleep. My irritated pores are burning, set aflame by my own salt, by the kind of sweat that only rage can press out. I turn on my heels, set on chasing the vanishing car; instead, I release a wail of desperation. The door of a nearby bar opens and a fat bald head peeks outside to check what's going on. I slump down on the pavement and stay there a long time, fifteen, twenty minutes maybe, after which I drag my battered body home.

I open the door with care and then rush inside, pulled in by a sudden surge of stench. Father is prostrated on the floor, his face immersed in the contents of his stomach. Through the soliloquy of gurgling, he's spitting out curses, our names, fragments of festival songs from the seventies. I take him under the arms, drag him to the bathtub, take his clothes off, give him a long shower. He squirms like a slug, unconsciously but with fortitude, then coughs up a handful of bile which obligingly goes down the drain. I dress him in his pajamas, tuck him in. I wake him up after an hour, give him some water and an aspirin. In the meantime, I scrub the living room floor, trying to exorcise the inexorable demons of nausea. After that I take out the trash: two empty liquor bottles; three handfuls of short, curly hairs; a bundle of smelly clothes. When I come back, I first check on Father's breathing. I step into the bathtub, stay much shorter than needed: all the warm water has been used on him. Shivering, I curl up under the bed sheets purchased when I was fifteen. I remember that well: Mother died shortly afterwards.

On the Bench

As I'm waiting for him to show up and sit next to me, I feel calm, superior to it all. My body is still plastered with bruises, but I suppose one could call it the price of growing up. The crowded heavens irradiate everything: people (visible, invisible); the tireless cicadas; the discordant salvos of the waves. Tingled pleasantly, sitting by myself for half an hour already, I'm closing in on the verses that have been slipping away from me for the past few evenings: *infinity, the grand hollow, white on black*. Before I'm able to grasp them, Father's shape emerges from the darkness, lead by the burning eye of a cigarette. I can tell that he was by the beach and then visited a neighbor or two: the smell of sweat has vanished, replaced by the scents of salt, tobacco, and freshly consumed wine spritzer. He sits next to me, on the bench hastily assembled ages ago to fit three people, which now squeals under our combined weight. He puts his arm over my shoulders and takes a long drag. The cigarette wakes up and illuminates his face, which seems to have aged twenty years overnight. I like that he's not starting a conversation. *What happened to you?* for example, or: *I stopped by the cemetery.*

BELMONDO

(for Ana)

The idea, he says, is simple: replace bad attitudes with good ones, the corrupting influence of modern times with an embrace of Mother Nature, and the desired change will come. I listen. I have no heart to tell him that I've been practicing attitude replacement for the past twelve months, and that all I achieved was stopping my moodiness from fermenting into chronic depression. As for Mother Nature, I've always been a fan: raw food, urinating by the trees, sunbathing and sea-bathing naked. However, I'm still where I am. You're missing the point, he says, as if reading my thoughts. You just came back from a kind of ordeal, your baseline is too low. Everyone's moody in the army. We should go camping, while it's still warm, just you and I. He keeps saying those things although it's seven in the morning, minutes after he picked me up at the station. I spent the night staring at the smudgy stars through a never-washed window, decoding variations in the rattling of the wheels, wondering what comes next. At least he's sober. That for sure counts as something.

When I wake up, it's almost time for lunch. The TV is on, but without the sound. He figured out, he says, that a droning human voice is what annoys him above anything else, plus everything one really needs can be gleaned from the images. As if responding to a secret pact between him and the airwaves, the screen unfolds footage that promises bright and warm days of early September: the sun is bouncing off the sea surface, failing to impress the old fisherman; the sheep are sleepy in verdant meadows; the pedestrians are delighted to cross the bridge. See, what did I tell ya, he gloats. A buddy of mine lent me his tent, we're leaving tomorrow morning. I sleepwalk through the apartment for the rest of the day, too confused to go out or call anyone. In the meantime, Father cooks, starts conversations that have nowhere to go, keeps taking bag after bag to the car. And this, he says, holding an elongated object wrapped in thick, camouflage-painted linen, is in case we need it. What is that, I ask. You know full well what this is, he says. Yes, but where did you get it? From a buddy of mine; he's a longtime party member, and they all got a piece and a box of ammunition per household. In case we run into wolves? Exactly, he says.

Judging by the patches of light on the curtains, the morning is as promised: luminous and calm. Father is already up, humming in the kitchen. I'm still somewhat confused by the change, by the softness of my own bed. Waking up, I even thought I caught a hint of Mother's scent, the evaporating warmth of her lips against my forehead. I stumble through the hallway, pause to look at the paintings on the wall. In two oils, a woman and a man are seated on a beach; in the third one, a woman holds a baby. In an aquarelle, three diffuse figures hurl shapeless snowballs at each other. By the time I'm at the table, Father has finished making scrambled eggs with prosciutto, something I haven't tasted since last summer. The door to the balcony is open. Morning noise is breezing in with the curtains. Are your ready, he asks. As ready as I'll be, I say.

In the car, we listen to a station that plays heart-distending potpourris of summer festivals and has no news until later in the afternoon. The windows are down, which lets in the reddish dust and sun-squeezed aromas of pine needles. I stick my head out and a hot, fragrant wind blasts my face. This must be what breaking the chrysalis feels like: the body still jammed in an enclosed space full of limbs, wings, camping gear, food, while the head catches glimpses of the world the way it is at that evanescent instant. We speak very little. I dare not ask whether there are any booze bottles in the trunk, Father dares not ask why I have no girlfriend. However, he does say: Did you see all those girls yesterday, waiting at the station?

After an hour or so of asphalt and gravel, we park on top of a hill sparsely covered with shrub. Much more impressive peaks are everywhere around us, as if the car capsized in a sea storm of rocks. Father spots a nice location for a tent: reasonably flat, covered with rare grass, locked between a pine copse and a gully that leads to a creek. Our own plumbing, to suit all our needs, he sings to a familiar yet unrecognizable tune, and we start unloading the car. The tent is up within half an hour, not least because what his buddy lent him is a small military model, apparently nicked during some maneuvers, and which I'm in full training to assemble. The last item in the car is the canvas sheet tube on the backseat floor. I unfold it and find a five-round semiautomatic rifle. I was assigned a Kalashnikov-style machine gun up until two days ago, but could handle this one with ease. Don't worry, it's not loaded, bullets are with me, shouts Father from the copse, his voice distorted through an effort that comes from squatting and contracting the abdomen.

After a lunch of canned meats and creek-chilled Coke (sometimes I'd kill for a beer, Father says), he decides that we should explore the area. I'm assigned to carry the weapon, he remains in charge of the bullets. For about an hour, the only animals in sight are the distant sheep, birds in flight, lizards sun-bathing on the rocks. We stay away from the rare houses and keep track of our route by memorizing trees. Three or four hours like this and we'd see the sea, Father says, pointing at the tallest range in sight, with two peaks rising above everything else: one with a monument, the other with a huge relay transmitter. The sun is moving closer to the jagged horizon, and we decide to get back to the camp. The moment we turn around Father stops and says, how about a rabbit for dinner? He points to a grayish furry rump some twenty meters away, half-concealed by a rock. Before I get a chance to offer an opinion, he gives me a sign to remain silent and hands me a bullet out of his breast pocket. One try, he whispers. I take off the rifle and load it. The soft clicking alerts our prey: it rears its head and lays its ears flat. I take aim, stop breathing, pull the trigger. A handful of dust bursts from the rock; the bang's echo spreads among the hilltops. You've got it, you've got it, he shouts, setting off to collect our meat. By the time we've reached the rock, however, there's no animal in sight, only crimson droplets that lead into dense bushes. Dinner for the foxes, Father says.

Back in the camp, we gather fallen branches for the fire. Father's still in high spirits. He points out that pine wood ignites quickly and is full of resin, which makes for these gorgeous, perfumed flames. We throw a few cans of beans into the hearth, then push them out, all ashen, a few minutes later. For a moment, all objects around us become extra-sharp and then quickly descend into darkness. The radio is on, set to the same feel-complicated station. (My joy, my sadness, my last and first love, sings a woman with a wailing vibrato.) Father must have timed our afternoon hike so as to miss the news. I ask him whether that was the case and he only shrugs. I sink a blade into a can, and a mouthful of hot beans sprays over my T-shirt.

Twice we've gone into the copse to collect more wood, which heats up fast and crackles and shoots up swirling colonies of sparkles. Father wants to know if I'm worried about college, how often I think I'll be able to visit, if anyone else from my class is going to Belgrade. I respond by admitting that this trip was an excellent idea. Who knows, maybe tomorrow we'll hunt something for real. I actually never tried rabbit meat. And it's been a while since I paid so much attention to the stars—it's nice to cultivate the sense of awe. Then I get up and step to the edge of the gully. Be careful, Father says to the sound of a few small rocks that start rolling down. Don't worry, I respond, dropping my pants. I probably never told you, but I really enjoy peeing in the open. From that vantage point one can see other fires, burning from afar.

I ask Father to tell me a story, just anything, something he never told me before. He's taken by surprise, and so am I. I like my needs guessed, not stated. Ever since Mother died, I say, you've been silent. As if you want to keep all memories of her to yourself. You were fifteen when she died, he replies; you should have plenty of memories. I need something that only the two of you knew; I want to be let in on a secret. A family secret, I add. Is that why you came to this trip, he asks—to talk about her? She sometimes pales from my mind, I say; I hate it when that happens. He's confused, keeps checking for something inside his jacket. The fire is crackling. Something akin to a song is coming from a distance. People like camping, he says. And then adds:

Shortly after we got married, I went on a business trip to Paris. Only on my last day did I have the time to walk the city. I bought a map, stepped into a metro for the first and last time in my life, got off close to the Boulevard Saint-Germaine. Then I entered a small labyrinth of pedestrian-only streets, walked into a few souvenir shops, bought her a scarf and an Eiffel Tower miniature. The crippled one that's on our TV set, I ask. I have to say, he goes on, I didn't feel like coming back. You may not like hearing it, but at the time I didn't like being married, to her or anyone else, and all of a sudden I'm in Paris. Why not stay there forever? It was early fall, the day was windy but as sunny and clear as this one, and I thought I felt truly happy for the first time in my life. However, every time I put my hands into the pockets of my outmoded trench coat, I'd feel the softness of the scarf or the edges of the Eiffel Tower and be overcome by the pointlessness of carrying them around. All of a sudden, I was awash with anger toward your mother. I stepped on the first bridge I saw, took out the scarf and let it fly out of my hand. I was about to get rid of the tower, too, but then I noticed a girl taking pictures of me doing crazy things and thought, well, what if I fell in love with her? Embarrassed by my anger, my outfit, my useless French, I waved clumsily in her direction and went back to walking the streets alone. I ate dinner in a small restaurant, did my best to look local. It was dark outside already, and my mood was darkening by the minute. In less than twelve hours, I was going to board a plane that would deliver me back into the life that, I was certain, I did not belong to. I decided to match the mood with scenery and observe the little of Paris I had left from below. I took the steps down to the river bank and started walking. It was much darker there than up on the street level, and the more I walked, the fewer people there were. I thought: What if something happened to me? What if I got robbed down here, or beaten, or killed? Would anyone ever know? Would the river drag me to the sea before anyone finds out? Then I noticed a commotion in the shadows, heard someone crying as if begging for mercy. I hesitated for a moment, then decided that I owed it to myself, to the city that has awaken me from the dead, to show some courage. I closed my fist around the Eiffel Tower, letting its sharp top protrude between the knuckles. I charged forward, yelling, releasing all my rage. There were three of them, surrounding a man on his knees, who was struggling to cover his head. I took them by surprise, jabbed the tip of my weapon into one guy's eye, then slashed the next one across his face. All three started to run. I threw the model into the Seine and approached the kneeling man, tried to help him get on his feet. At that moment, two policemen jumped me and I hit the ground, my ears abuzz with the shock. Then the man spoke, and the policemen retreated and apologized. They called someone on the radio and within minutes two police cars were parked on the bridge above. The man insisted that they give us a ride in the same vehicle. His face was sprayed with blood, but seemed to be without wounds. He smiled at me and I thought that I had met him before. In the car, he was dictating something to an officer, then signed some papers. *Yougoslavie*, I kept saying, still confused, whenever they looked at me, *Yougoslavie*. When we stopped in front of a pristine white building with wrought iron gates, the man waved me to get out as well. *Bonne soirée, Monsieur Belmondo,* one of the policemen said, and they drove away. Thank you, Mister, said Jean-Paul Belmondo. You probably saved my life. Do you speak English?

Fighting disbelief, I managed to explain that I speak very little French and no English at all. I also accepted an invitation to come upstairs. It was one of his several apartments in Paris, he said, or at least that's what I understood, and the one closest to the party he needed to go to. We need to go, he added, moving his hand to and fro between us. At the door, we were greeted by a middle-aged maid, who hurried us into the kitchen and started attending to bruises on his face and small wounds on my hand. We then took showers and I was given a change of his clothes. Some ridiculous photos came flashing back, of me and my buddies posing like Belmondo from the movies. My favorite pose was the one from *Breathless*—the way he moved his lips with his thumb; did you ever see that one?

The maid was studying me with an intense suspicion, but my host was very relaxed about everything. We even had a glass of cognac before we left. A black Citröen was waiting outside. In the car, we didn't talk much but he smiled every now and then, saying stuff like *Yougoslavie, tres, tres bien*—I guess things he hoped I'd understand. Soon, we were in front of another elegant residence. From the street, one could see a huge bubbly party happening on the first level. On our way in, everyone was greeting him and wondering who the hell I was. The first thing I noticed was a live jazz quartet, playing in a corner. Belmondo looked around and, before I had a chance to get a drink, steered me toward a window where a skinny man with a dark bushy mane was standing, a glass of liquor in one hand and cigarette in another, surrounded by a cluster of chatty Parisian girls. I envied him immediately. At the sight of Belmondo, the girls made room and Jean-Paul introduced me to

Danilo Kiš. The two of them exchanged a few inaudible words, with Jean-Paul patting me on the back. He must have told Kiš how brave I was. He then shook my hand, said *merci* once more, and disappeared into the crowd. Kiš was polite, guessed immediately where I was from, asked what I was doing in Paris. It turned out that we had a few mutual acquaintances in Cetinje. I was embarrassed that I'd heard of him but never read any of his books. He did seem anxious to get back to the conversation he was having with those girls, and they were buzzing around us constantly, reminding me that I did not belong there. I said goodbye and went back to the black Citröen, where I changed into my old clothes. The chauffeur even took me to my hotel. The next day, at the airport, I bought another Eiffel Tower. When I got home, I realized how much I missed your mother. As I was running up the stairs, my only gift from Paris in my hand, I slipped and fell. That's why the thing on our TV set has only three legs.

You're lying, that's what's you're doing. You're making things up, you're not telling me anything again, there's no way she would have kept a story like this one secret. She was confiding in me, telling me everything, you're a liar, I'm about to tell him. I stay silent, however, because his face drops and he suddenly looks a decade older, and it's not clear whether that's an effect of the story or an illusion brought about by the dying fire. Then a wolf howls and a branch snaps in the copse. Father reaches for the gun, fumbles through his breast pocket, loads the container with three shiny bullets. At the next cracking sound, he fires twice in the air. The cracking stops, and so do songs in the distance.

After we've searched around with flashlights, the rifle ready, we both step to the edge of the gully and urinate into the darkness below. By the time we're in the tent, I lose the will to protest against the abject fiction I was told. The station is about to broadcast midnight news, and Father hurries to turn the radio off. Both tired, we don't bother saying good night. Sleep takes me swiftly and brings no dreams.

I take that back. Right before opening my eyes, I do hear steps and an excited murmur of a crowd, and then there's this elegant, brightly lit apartment full of happy, intoxicated people, among them Mother, dancing with abandon, while Father is changing his clothes in a corner. His lips are coarse, resting against a flask that protrudes from his jacket, and the air is saturated with a strong smell of liquor. The steps and voices are growing louder, and I see human shadows, curious and sharp, crawling up the tent.

As I turn to Father to wake him up, someone rips open the entrance and pulls me outside. I see men in uniform, who now barge in and pull out Father, who tries but can't protect his eyes from the morning sun. Who the fuck are you, says an unshaven, middle-aged lieutenant. With Father busy finding his bearings, I try to explain that we're just campers, father and his out-of-army son, trying to reconnect and catch the last days of summer. Don't lie to me, you motherfucker, says the officer. Were you spying on us? Were you? At that moment, an equally unshaven soldier gets out of the tent, carrying our rifle. And what's this, the lieutenant says, grabbing the weapon from the soldier's arms. Father and I exchange panicked looks, which makes the case against us particularly damning. The soldiers scurry away from the line of fire, leaving us in the middle of a crescent, facing the lieutenant, who's now aiming alternately between our chests. If you're so scared, it means the gun is loaded, he says triumphantly. While we're on our way to kick Croats' asses, you motherfuckers are sneaking up on us with your camouflage tent and a loaded gun. We sink to our knees in fear. He then lowers the barrel, pulls the magazine open, and the remaining bullet flies out, like a stunned bumblebee. This solidifies our guilt, and Father's insistence to talk to a superior, use a field phone, send a homing pigeon only enrages the lieutenant further. They tie our arms, throw us back into the tent, and make a fence around it out of pine spikes they carved from the copse trees. Then they start cutting down more branches, singing songs of redemption and slaughter, telling jokes about firing squads and women.

A few hours later, a colonel with his entourage will drive by and grant us our freedom. We'll pack our stuff in haste. Giving me the gun back, the lieutenant will advise me not to fool around, to report for duty promptly when the summons for reserve arrives. Your country is your mother, he'll say. Never forget that.

REARRANGEMENTS

(for Svetlana Lukić and Svetlana Vuković)

True or not, I credit the two of us, Kate and myself, for developing the whole concept of cryptofucking. It would go like this: on any given propitious occasion—an unseasonably warm evening like this one, for example, after meeting at the station and almost colliding with a young, solemn-looking couple dragging their instruments (she a cello, he a contrabass)—Kate and I would enter a conversation, swift and vertiginous, which would take us home and be followed by food on the table and drinks in our glasses, and then by more talking and some undressing, by desserts and kissing and grating of our nipples against the ripples of bed covers, and then by grabbing and twisting and suckling, by sampling the flesh of fruit, of pillows, of ourselves, by arguing, intensely, on many a topic, and finally by coming, simultaneously, to a conclusion that we've fucked each other's brains out whilst pretending that we were doing something else.

True or not, I say, although in this case the truth will likely never be known. What can be said with certainty: it's early March here by the lake, a mere two weeks after the last serious snowstorm, and against all expectations the spring has come, with its measles of brilliant green on every tree and the violet pus trumpets bubbling from the still grey earth. And yes: bugs are afloat everywhere, the unrelenting clouds of winged dandelion seeds, and a gaze averted skyward, in an attempt to evade yet another swarming pillow, will bring no relief, unless relief can be found in a sight of heavy bulbs of white and purple hanging from bare branches, ready for unfolding, February-in-New-Orleans style. The spring indeed, I told myself this morning, and then, in the afternoon, while waiting for the train, almost got drenched by an august and honest July shower. In the evening, even the sun seemed out of season, deep red and swollen, going down with a protracted descent, like an inflamed tonsil. At the station, Kate sees me all weak and disoriented, under the spell of springtime malaise, and moves quickly from underneath the canopy to pull me away from the tracks, lest I fall to my death, pushed there by an innocent, solemn-looking couple of musicians dragging their instruments—she a cello, he a contrabass—in their shiny casings. It also can be said, with utmost confidence, that truth cannot be found in disease-tinted descriptions of the seasons, nor does it lie in the bliss and rescue maneuvers a young marriage brings.

∞

My birthplace is elsewhere. I used to call it, with adolescent conviction, Macondo, Buenos Aires. Over there, springs remain forever majestic, complicated, slightly nauseating. All summers are identical, too: replete with unrequited loves on a windy beach, the climaxes of mirthful, crazy sorrows. You can tell the fall has come by the skin flaking off girls' shoulders, by suntan vanishing in patches from their faces, by yet another half-consumed love affair of mid-level schooling. And each winter is short, so short and incomplete that its only purpose seems to be in being sobering and forgettable. Once high school is over, the military service is due: a year-long excuse from reality filled with books, pitiful attempts at poetry, and extraordinary masturbatory efforts—all manifestations of a boy's epic struggle with himself. As soon as the boy takes off his uniform, the war, a real one, begins.

A good part of my freshman year is spent in the attic of a turn-of-the-century building, adjacent to the city's Philharmonic Orchestra Hall. My desiccated professor of vertebrate zoology—her face already resembling its own skull, her skeleton showing in great detail through the gauze of once fashionable blouses—sits by an open window and strains her tiny voice, sometimes with passion, fighting back the orchestra in midst of their tuning sessions and rehearsals. Her squeals for attention are either blasted away by the sounds of Brahms and Beethoven or muffled by the aromas of *capriciosa*, *quattro staggioni*, *calzone*, wafting from somewhere nearby straight into our minds, already clouded by the pungent marinade of formalin in which the overused specimens on our tables have been served. One day in early October, after a highly confusing lecture on circulatory systems (our hearts felt far less regulated than the lesson implied), I step for the first time into a narrow passageway between our building and the Orchestra Hall. That pizza place must be somewhere here, says my irritated nose, and sure enough, there's a door into the unknown, bearing the name of Verdi and a shiny, greasy logo: a musical clef, melting into a steaming piece of dough.

The restaurant downstairs is spacious, an impression enhanced by the fact that only two of about two dozen tables are occupied: one by the entrance, by a young man finishing off his pizza and beer, and the next one by four musicians and their instruments—one cello, two violins, a horn—in their tattered cases. Soft Yugoslav pop from the early eighties oozes from the speakers (Your beast loves you, yes, he loves you, sings a man with a bad cold), and the air is thick with promise of a hot meal, reasonably priced. As I step in, no one looks in my direction, not even the two bald, thick-necked waiters at the bar, their eyes fixed upon something at their feet, their shiny foreheads almost touching. Small-time thugs released on probation, pronounces a voice in my head, and the thought, stirred up by anxieties of a freshman from the province and augmented by his formidable hunger, develops by itself: pizzeria Verdi is just a front for organized crime, a clearinghouse for ex-convicts, an establishment that matches patently inhospitable people with the hospitality industry. Not liking the place but starving and cash-strapped, I hurry to a table that seems the least exposed to everyone's sight. A small window above my head rises up to a knees' height above the pavement outside, which allows for monitoring of the passing boots and skirted female thighs. This makes me forget for a while the hunger and the snake pit I entered.

Whaddaya want? says the smaller and sturdier of the two, in a subdued voice, appearing from behind my back. A calzone and a Heineken, please, I reply in my best pleasant-neutral tone, which is met with a probing silence. I bet he has no idea what a calzone is. I eschew eye contact, lest I provoke uncorking of my throat with the bottle opener dangling from his apron. It works: he shuffles off to the bar, picks up a telephone, and relates something unintelligible to whoever is listening. After a long, silent look exchanged with his partner, he reaches for the bottle opener and starts scraping clean the undersides of his fingernails.

I want to leave, badly, but don't dare, now that I've ordered and gotten myself involved in a highly precarious situation. So I go back to staring through the window and then shift my focus, slowly, to people in the room. My waiter's nowhere to be seen. The other one is busy flattening a few crumpled bills with his chunky fingers, which I bet acquired their distorted shape in fist fights and are kept strong and flexible by regular acts of strangulation. The young man seated by the entrance does not seem scared, but rather exhausted beyond any measure: he counts his change slowly, leaves what has to be a very small tip, gets up as if burdened by a backpack filled with stones, and leaves his table limping. The musicians must be relieved that he's gone, because their conversation picks up in speed and volume almost instantly. Even so, I can hear only useless fragments from where I'm sitting, words like *orchestra* or *Norway* or *France*. They've got to be talking about their upcoming tour; less plausibly, they could be playing a game of words containing letters r and a. Having figured that out, I find myself envying them profoundly: they're about to leave this basement of a country, or at least find out who has a superior vocabulary. The war has begun, everyone says so, and everyone, Father included, is pondering everyone else's exit strategies. I'm glad you never wanted to become a lawyer, he says, as I'm boarding a train to Belgrade that will pull me out of his life like an annoying extra tooth. It would have been even worse, he shouts, craning his neck, trying to impart yet another bit of parental wisdom to his college-bound son, if you'd chosen to become a... Since it's unlikely we'll ever revisit the topic, there's no damage in those last words being lost to the sounds of the engine, to the essences of sweat emanating off my fellow passengers.

There's no purpose in bringing out the zoology textbook and pretending to read it: the unholy spirits of formalin could detach from its pages and ruin my disguise. My strategy still based on remaining unnoticed, I stare at an empty plate with head in my hands, alternately faking headache and deep thinking. After a while I give up, go to the musicians' table, and ask if I could join them. Of course, says the youngest of the four, and moves his chair so I can squeeze in. The others nod in an unconvincing agreement, exchanging looks that at least do not appear hostile. It turns out that my spying efforts were misguided: the words that had caught my ear were neither a game nor fragments of an itinerary. Norway is the country where more and more musicians from Belgrade Philharmonic Orchestra seek work, and France is where the town of Vézelay is. As the youngest of the quartet was just explaining—By the way, my name is David, he says *en passant*—that town has an abbey with apparently superb acoustics. Rostropovich himself chose it to record the cello suites by Bach, after decades of searching. Do you know that music, David asks looking me in the eyes, and all I can answer is that I'm familiar with both names. Pushed by an itching silence that follows my admission of ignorance, I offer an anecdote of Mother bringing a bag full of LPs from her trip to Bari, Italy (instead of buying more Italian clothes, Father complained), and of her listening to one in particular, featuring Rostropovich, up until the vinyl ridges got barely readable. (Father also complained about the constant brooding uhmm-dada-uhm-dam.) Which piece exactly, do you remember, David asks again, which resurrects a long-forgotten image of Mother smiling, holding an LP sleeve in one hand and a cup of coffee in the other, a column of cigarette smoke smearing metallic gray hues over her natural pallor. The sleeve is light blue, with a black-and-white photo of the maestro emerging from the background, embracing his instrument as if about to abduct it into darkness or twist its neck in an act of passion. The cover announces, in large white letters, MSTISLAV ROSTROPOVIČ INTERPRETA, and then in yellow and somewhat smaller font, DVOŘÁK, Concerto per violoncello op. 104. I thank the quartet for finding interest in my mother's taste (letting the image linger in my mind, avowing silently to revisit it soon), and even share that, for me, the said concerto has a moment so powerful and beautiful that I always thought of it as "mind-blowing," long before I learned the word and started using it in conjunction with guitar solos of Jimmy Hendrix and Mark Knopfler. Let me guess, says David, picking up the cello from its case. After a few adjustments (the chair, the instrument, his lanky body), not paying attention to his older colleagues and their rolling eyeballs, he indeed plays the part I'm thinking of: the several bars that burst into an ascending scale executed at the speed of a fast and heavy inhale, only to dissolve into an eruption of the imagined orchestra. David plays it well, and the orchestra part actually starts booming in my head, not like a memory, but like a total physical evocation. I must have even tried to form the melody with my clumsy vocal cords, because David stops and everyone is staring at me.

The rush of blood into my cheeks does not prevent me from sensing that something hot is breathing by my ear. After a moment or two, the source of heat shifts: my waiter extends his pumped-up arm and drops a round, steaming calzone almost in my lap, saying, Here, one for you. Hey, buddy, why don't you play us some more? says the other waiter, carrying five beer bottles plugged in between his mighty knuckles. Yeah, why don't you? echoes my waiter and slaps me on the shoulder, as if offering fulfillment of a lifelong wish. Driven by some kind of instinct reserved for policemen and bouncers, the two of them move side to side and lean on our table with their fists, revealing a jagged storyline of their forearms: voluptuous women in polka dot bikinis;

knives dripping pale-blue blood; three-headed snakes, their fangs moist with poison; boat anchors and five-pointed stars, illegibly dated. David shoots me a smile, as if my life, not his, depends on pleasing our captors. This, my friends, he says, is by Johann Sebastian Bach: Sarabande from the Cello Suite No. 2, in D-minor. As the great Rostropovich put it once, it's for those who've known sadness. Cut the bullshit and play, says my waiter. Yeah, says the other. David draws a long breath and, on exhale, a dry and sweet hum full of longing permeates the room.

The next day, both government and opposition outlets keep silent about two dangerous criminals being dissolved into non-existence in a downtown basement restaurant. Less surprisingly, there are also no accounts of David and me going to his studio nearby, starting and finishing a bottle of cheap red, and making it to a jazz club afterwards, two blocks down the street, where more wine and some vodka is consumed. No surprise either that there's no mention of me waking up on David's floor, fully dressed, dragging my face across the carpet and into the bathroom, where an urge to expel something viscous and purple through my facial orifices is relieved before I'm able to reach the toilet bowl. And of course, everyone ignores the fact that I spend a long, long time cleaning up and resisting another gastrointestinal mayhem, upon which I step out of the bathroom, refreshed and somewhat stabilized, with a small towel wrapped around my hips. My pitiful bundle of clothes is jammed into a double garbage bag, and I can't decide whether its stench really expands beyond its PVC barrier or if it all is just in my nostrils. David is awake on an expandable sofa, stark naked, unable to peel away his bloodshot eyes from the TV. A town riddled with bullets and grenades is crumbling into its pixilated self as the announcer lists heroic achievements of the Yugoslav People's Army, whose brave and resourceful soldiers finally liberated the beautiful municipality of Vukovar. David pulls his knees up to his chin and starts rocking back and forth, releasing an incomprehensible sequence of murmurs and growls. Not able to get to him, I go through his clothes without asking and change into a pair of washed out jeans size too tight for me and a shirt claiming that Dead Can Dance. Getting naked and dressed in the middle of his one-room abode, I realize with relief that his red eyes are now shut tightly. I did nothing wrong, there's nothing to be ashamed of, I keep saying to myself.

A week later I knock on David's door, his clean clothes in my backpack, a lengthy apology on my lips. He cuts my speech short and waves me inside. The sofa bed is folded and he's not naked anymore, but with the TV turned way up, with his eyes red and swollen, he looks as if he's woken up in the morning from a week ago. The air is stale and infused with many a repelling sensation, traces of my vomiting extravaganza included. I open the door to a small balcony, and David recoils from the chill and street noise that barge in. Would you like to go out and have breakfast, I ask, and he nods in agreement that comes from an absence of will to resist. Bags of assorted bread rolls in our pockets, we cross the Kalemegdan Park and lean on the fortress walls that overlook the misty confluence of the Sava and the Danube. The horizon is close, just beyond the banks, with the Pannonian plains evaporating into fog that turns, seamlessly, into a monolayer of clouds.

The long, numbing silence is broken by David, who recounts events so improbable and twisted that for a moment I have no questions to ask. He then proclaims to have flown to that same corner of the fortress for the past few nights, disguised as Pablo Casals in drag. Each time he did that, he'd deposit a coin in a mounted spyglass the shape of a mortar and observe his parents' bodies floating down the Sava.

By December, I barely manage to keep up with my lecture-and-lab schedule while attending David's tryouts and concerts. We have lunches together in greasy, nausea-inducing eateries for students and blissfully drink the weeknights away, inhaling the smoky air of jazz clubs, where he's occasionally invited onstage and invariably cheered on by a small yet enthusiastic cohort of jazz groupies. Here and there I wake up on his fragile sofa and leave silently, while the David-girl combo of the night snores entangled in a mess of bed sheets on the floor.

It's my first trip back, and Father welcomes me at the railway station. He hasn't shaved since September and must have cut on bathing, too. The rumor has it, he says, that the state-run company where he works is about to fold, and that they're all heading the route of early retirement. Although, he says, it all must be a conspiracy to push him out, those goddamn marauders, to do that to him, the most qualified, the only decent one of the lot. As we walk home, I start wondering whether his paranoia and the attempts to conceal his trembling hands are harbingers of an impending delirium tremens; his announcement, in a shaky voice, that he quit drinking once and for all makes me tremble as well. I spend the first night awake, making frequent stops to the room that used to be theirs, listening in on his spasms and nightmares. In the lifting darkness, it dawns on me that the place is losing signs of my existence, just like it happened with mother's. My room is now being used as storage for wine bottles, and all that's left of her are a few paintings, their frames spliced with the graying walls.

Father downs two shots of grappa before breakfast, which has an immediate calming effect on his nerves. He even takes a lengthy bath. We get into the car and drive to Virpazar. The day is sunny and calm, warm enough that his buddy the restaurant owner gives us a table on the patio, right by the lake. We make it through a few pounds of smoked bleak salad and a few liters of house red with ease. By the time walnut crackers and Turkish coffee arrive, it almost feels like the summer five years ago, with the three of us at this same table, on our way to the seaside. Son, says Father after an extra-long digestive silence, your summons for the army reserve came the other day. They're not supposed to do it, bastards, you're a registered college student, I told them. I tore it apart, told them motherfuckers you don't live here anymore.

V spots us coming from afar and keeps waving until we're parked in front of the house. The seaside is even warmer, with the sea barely audible and glistening in the winter sun. She hugs us fiercely, asks son, what's with all that beard, and Father just shrugs and steps inside the house. I start telling her about my new life, but those two worlds, the college and V's patio, seem hopelessly distant and immiscible. Your father told me about the summons, she says. Don't you dare report for duty. If must be, she adds with a grin, come back here and camp out on the beach; you know only we could ever find you there. We make it back to the city in time for the evening news. Fuck all this, Father says at the first sight of a shaky footage of blasts, moans, and blood-soaked bandages. Good she's not alive to see it.

The following week I spend with friends from high school. It turns out that some of them don't mind the whole bloody shebang. It's about time the scores are settled, they say. I knew nothing of the scores, I respond, half-drunk. Wait until Bosnia blows up, they say. Five hundred years we've been under their heel, five hundred years. Then everybody counts down from ten, roars in approval, and starts kissing everybody else. You must come by the church for the Orthodox Christmas Eve, they say; it's gonna be a helluva party.

Put on a furlough, with his retirement imminent indeed, Father spends the first days of nineteen-ninety-two on the couch, deeply immersed in alcoholic vapors. I don't know where to go, stuck between his drunken diatribes and the city that has simultaneously turned violently mad and hopelessly depressive. Long evening walks my only refuge, I take to the streets regularly, with a formidable goal of discovering routes where I won't meet anyone I know. On Christmas Eve, however, an enormous crowd sucks me in and drags me to the plateau underneath the church, where the metropolitan and a strange red-haired man, both in black robes, stand surrounded by armed men in camouflage attire, their guns aloft. As shots in the air die down, and as the metropolitan begins his oration (the red-haired man taking a step back from the microphone), I squeeze out of the mass into a dark abandoned graveyard. That tricky maneuver renders me completely alone, away from the crowd that has begun chanting about joys of Christmas and fratricide, shielded by nothing more than a row of cypresses and the fear of open tombs. A brief spell of dizziness sends me onto a slab of concrete covered with moss and lichen; while recovering my strength, I try to read the eroded name with my fingers. I then hurry home, eager to announce that I'm leaving first thing in the morning. Where the fuck do you think you're goin', father asks, lying prostrate, face to face with his shadows.

∞

My college schedule soon becomes overwhelming. I still feel a need to be around David, but not when he's all red-eyed and moody or fucking someone under my nose, which is almost every time we meet up. In addition, almost resigned to the prospect of not being able to find a girlfriend, I deliberately start withdrawing into the black hole of my curriculum. Our encounters are farther and farther apart and, by the time my sophomore year begins, we're not able to talk with ease anymore. In the meantime, Bosnia did blow up as announced. On TV, war reportage is tastefully mixed with brain-splitting folk music and shows with seers who cure cancer on the spot, even in relatives from war-ravaged regions.

Then, in the summer of ninety-four, I undergo an unexpected crash course in sexual healing, exhilaration, and heart amputation at the hands of an Asian-American who ventured to our fractured land to practice peace, love, and misunderstanding. In desperation, I grow a beard and start consuming copious amounts of father's favorites, until one day David spots me staggering around the building where I first heard the sounds of Belgrade

Philharmonic Orchestra, unable to remember which classes to attend. He takes me up in his apartment and, after a week or so of domestic care, our friendship and my self-restraint around bottles are restored. On the final day of my rehab, while examining my hairy self in the mirror, I realize that finally there's a larger project worth pursuing: (1) shave; (2) finish the studies as soon as possible; (3) find a way to America; (4) locate the girl on the run with my heart in her backpack.

Focused and determined, I refuse to succumb to the war, poverty, and whatever else is out there. I visit father rarely, try to ignore the sprawling disarray of his life. Inspired by David's side career of a wedding & jazz club & you-name-the-occasion-and-venue musician, I start giving chemistry lessons to medical students and soon declare, to father's astonishment, my fragile financial independence. I still don't get to hang out much with David, but this time it's by design and free from awkward pauses. The best of all: I maintain a stable flow of girlfriends. Here and there, I almost feel in love.

∞

The short winter days are grueling, with fog and soot stuffing up the air, with cracked skin on the back of my hands, and danger lurking everywhere. I wake up in a student dormitory, in nearly complete darkness. My shoes are heavy with yesterday's mud, their thick laces full of melted snow. The city bus is a noisy cube of chill, reeking of too a successful Saturday night. The lab is empty—of course: it's Sunday, 8 a.m.—and even colder than the bus. I spend hours working hard with no breakfast, with fingers aching from cold, with a lab coat forced over my best and only jacket. Mocking my precautions, acid burns start popping up on its surface and the finest goose down emerges, as the label suggested it would. Outside, the noise is rising steadily: more and more people are passing by the building, carrying flags and painted slogans, banging on pots, calling politicians names. It hits me then that Hana must be waiting for me, that I better hurry up. As I reach for the frosty door handle, I realize in horror that the solutions it took me the entire morning to concoct got somehow mixed up, thus rendering my three-week efforts useless— unless I figure out, right now, what's in each bottle and reapply everything to backup samples. I pick up the phone and call Hana's home. She's out already, her mother says, not hiding her disapproval of everything and everyone her daughter is involved in and with. I can't leave the lab now, it'd take much more time to get to this point if I left, there's no justification for impeding scientific progress and my own graduation efforts in the name of a promising romance and lofty political goals. I crank up volume on the gramophone, the only item in the lab that makes my life bearable, to an apparent delight of Ms Grace Jones, who, finally liberated, testifies with gusto that love is a drug and that life can be *en rose*.

Thanks to a state of heightened awareness (physical exertion plus mental strain plus hunger equals sharp and unrelenting focus, at least for a while), looking for Hana in a river of people turns into a mini-detective project with a happy ending. I first assume, with great confidence, that she did wait for me, but no longer than fifteen minutes, upon which she decided to join the protesters, as was our intention anyway, and that, given her unshakeable political beliefs and tremendous ease in conversing with strangers, she has not stopped marching and chanting ever since. In other words, in order to make a good guess of her whereabouts at this particular moment, all it takes is to estimate the speed at which the river of people is flowing and cross that information with the route of the march, broadcasted on opposition radio stations all morning. Then a mad dash begins, along shortcuts, through the equation for speed that keeps turning in my head, reminding me to factor in Hana's movement as well. Finally, I rejoin the crowd at pretty much exact spot she reaches a few moments later, whistle in her mouth, red carnival hat on her head, exchanging indecisive glances with a guy on her left. I swoop in with kisses, apologies, vague avowals that guarantee nothing but imply together forever.

The day suddenly feels good: we walk and chant, hand in hand, for a few good hours, throw eggs at the Departments of Interior and Exterior, size up police squadrons on sidewalks, scream occasionally at the top of our lungs: Murderers! Thieves! Traitors! The crowd takes us back to the lab building and we step aside, our minds clear, our bodies ready. On our way in, we run into mayor-elect Đinđić and his good-looking wife. It's no wonder we meet them: he essentially runs the protests and lives nearby. What makes an impression is the absence of any security detail. What a guy, Hana says; imagine him running the country, instead of this gang of killers and marauders.

We tiptoe into the darkness of the lab, lock the door behind us, and open the one leading into my professor's office. His large walnut desk is covered with papers and family photos. Hana turns everything into neat stashes and puts it carefully away, then unbuttons her blouse. We do it quickly, right there, on the desk, under the streetlamp light sliced up by out-of-synch blinds. As her body relaxes and begins to twitch, and as my own mind begins to cloud with slumber, the radiators unexpectedly begin to hiss, reminding me of the bitter winter we're in. I pull my molting jacket over our naked bodies, bruised and battered by love under harsh circumstances. The twitches I fall into are so strong that they wake me up, long enough to realize that I'm starving, that we'll need to get off the desk and leave before dawn.

The winter is long, and people keep taking to the streets. The police squadrons are hitting with passion now, sharing their workload with private armies of thugs who wield long sticks and profess no mercy. There have been rumors that Đinđić's assassination is a matter of days, but he still shows up in the open. Hana and I are pressing against each other in front of the Film Museum, awaiting Jack Nicholson in *Carnal Knowledge*. The program says the subtitles are in Czech, which, David says, should be much fun. It's been a while, he adds, coming out of nowhere, grabbing my shoulder from behind. I turn around and first see a red-haired girl with huge glasses hanging by his arm, looking sleepy and bemused at the same time. This is Nataša, David says, and I check them both out: without those glasses and with less unruly hair, she'd pass for very pretty; David seems to have lost weight since our last encounter (when was that?), so it takes some time to recognize the pair of jeans I once borrowed from his apartment. This is David, my cellist friend, I say. Oh, how interesting, says Hana stretching out her hand, still warm from our embrace. In the theater, we laugh hard: not because of sexual transgressions of Jack Nicholson and Art Garfunkel, but because of those Czech subtitles, which turn each phrase into something that sounds like accidentally corrupted Serbo-Croatian. The great Slav brotherhood is one great misunderstanding, says David with a whisper, and both girls giggle softly.

After the show, David suggests that we all go to his apartment. My hunger for Hana is enormous and I start looking for excuses, but they are all trounced by her passion for meeting new people. His place is the same, save for boxes upon boxes of sheet music piled up against the only accessible wall. The fridge is largely vacant, but Nataša and I team up and very soon the plates are on the table, with a reasonably appealing variation on the ham-and-eggs theme in each. Meanwhile, David has taken out his cello and Hana cannot conceal her enthusiasm for his bowing technique. We're together for almost six months— how about you, asks Nataša, almost inaudible through the flood of trills and arpeggios that spread from the living-fucking room. About the same, I reply, but with a feeling of just having told a lie. I think David mentioned you a few times; how come we've never met? I'm in the lab all the time. Did you know he's been there once? Where exactly? To Vukovar. Where? To Vukovar, to look for his parents, she repeats with a shout, but the music has already stopped. Let's leave fun talk for after dinner, David says, beads of sweat on his forehead, and pours us each a glass of some cheap red. It was the Humoresque by Rostropovich that he played, exclaims Hana, pink in the face.

After we've drained our second bottle and every other topic—politics, sports, professor-on-student gossip—I seize a sudden spell of silence and ask that David tell the story of his trip to Vukovar. The silence solidifies, and I force my gaze upon the rim of my glass. No more bowing tonight, passes through my mind, after which I mutter a weak sorrynevermind. No, no, says David, his voice shaking with alcohol-fortified defiance. After all, he says, it's a good one, with a happy ending. My hand looks for Hana's under the table, but all it finds is her cold and reproachful grip. David opens yet another bottle and straightens up in his chair. I still don't dare look up, but judging by the angle of his torso, his eyes are resting on Hana.

It was briefly after Miloš and I met, he begins. When he woke up on my floor one morning and left for the bathroom, I turned on the TV and saw my hometown in ruins, something I knew was underway but had been only imagining till then. I even thought I saw my parents hiding behind a crumbled wall that could have been the one surrounding our yard. But I was horrified and hung over, and Miloš was vomiting his guts out, and I just didn't know what to do or think. A few mornings later, I made it across the border with a plan to get to the town posing as a paramilitary volunteer. One *četnik* and his girlfriend intercepted my march through corn fields and asked for an ID. No ID, I replied. The Croats burned down my house, I said, serving them a tale prepared on the way: life in a nearby Serb village, Croatian police storming the house in the middle of the night, family dead, me narrowly escaping after wrestling down the schoolboy who was guarding me. They saw a copy of a *četnik* weekly in my pocket, recognized my local accent, and decided to believe me. Then they gave me an unmarked uniform and let me spend the night in their tent. In the morning, they said, my training will begin: a couple of captives needed to be taken care of. With some luck, said the girlfriend, as three of us lay on thin mattresses that wafted of beer and urine, those will be the same bastards who slaughtered your folks. They were both snoring within minutes, so sneaking out in the middle of the night was the easy part. As I entered the city limits I hit a wall of stench, which I knew was rising from the decomposing flesh around me. Nose in my collar, relying on a few remaining landmarks and counting street corners in the moonlight, I found my house, half-obliterated, but with no bodies around. At dawn, I made a decision to stay, wait the siege out, and then continue looking for my parents. Soon thereafter, a unit of bearded men found me asleep on a mound of rubble and woke me up with kicks. In uniform and unarmed, lurking beyond enemy lines, I couldn't pass for one of theirs, so they took me in as an enemy combatant. I can tell a Croat by the face, boasted their superior, grinning with confidence, and added that I should not hope for a prisoner swap. They put me together with a group of people that stuck together like penguins in snow storm. Luckily, I recognized no one. After a while, hours maybe, they separated women from men; being the youngest, I was sure they were going to shoot me first. I started thinking about the couple who let me in their tent last night, whether they'll be the ones to do it. Then two women showed up out of nowhere, elbowing their way through loose gangs of armed, intoxicated men, microphones in their hands. One was interviewing a colonel who seemed all too proud to talk to the press, while the other was snooping around, taking notes. I don't know how it happened, but my eyes locked with the note taker. She halted, hesitated for an instant, and then walked straight to our guard, pointing in my direction and shouting that I'm with them. She dropped a name—Lazar! Lazar Milić!—and I realized that I should pretend it's mine. Within seconds, both women were all over the colonel, explaining something about the "guide," "homeless," "local boy," gesticulating vigorously in my direction. I guess everyone believes you when you're acting the right amount of crazy. I got extracted from the group, didn't dare looking back. The two women burst into fits of sobbing and hugging, wondering out loud how in the world we got separated. Within thirty minutes, we were speeding away in their car, making it to Belgrade by night, a handwritten note from the colonel taking us through checkpoints. The strangest thing: I have some of it on video.

David pops a cassette into his VCR and, after some whirring, a familiar scene unfolds: ruined houses, bodies by a ditch that a solemn voice identifies as "our slaughtered kin." The scene then cuts to a wounded young soldier, neatly shaven and baby-faced, who claims to regret all the innocent victims but remains determined to defend his country. At the end of the interview one can see them, three hurried specks, traversing a corner of the screen and getting into a car. How come you never told me about him, about all this, Hana says, her puffy eyes full of indignation.

A few weeks later, Hana and I break up, agreeing that we could—hey, should, why not?—stay friends. It stings that not long afterward she hooks up with David and that I have to endure their joint presence, hand holding and all, in the third-row seats that David had secured before our rearrangements took place. As I squirm and fidget and look nowhere in particular, a thunderous applause halts the barbed, stunted words that are about to leave my mouth and I see the maestro march across the stage with the gait of an overjoyed, oversized child. The announcer welcomes Mstislav Rostropovich and an esteemed Italian chamber orchestra. Before I get a chance to consciously stop throwing furtive glances at David and Hana or tune out two candy-unwrapping machines seated right behind me, the music—a Baroque piece I remember no longer—rises like a tide of thousand forgotten embraces and lifts me up, all the way to the ceiling of the enormous concert hall. For an entire hour I float there, immersed in music like amniotic fluid, mindful of every vibration that enters my earlobes. Finally, I relinquish control of my facial muscles as my senses turn inward, searching for resonances between the eardrums and what some insist should be called the soul. As an encore, as David had guessed he would, the maestro plays one of Bach's suites. I hear David whisper something quickly to Hana, but I'm not interested in their sweet talk anymore. My mind cleared, all of a sudden governed by an instinct that resides, pulsating and warm, in my every organ, I don't wait for the final applause to simmer down or for David and Hana to ask why I got up so abruptly. I rush out of the concert hall and take a two-hour-long walk to my place through a biting winter night, each step reverberating with what some would call meaning, awakening, insight. The next day I print out a handful of application forms, call father, and tell him that I need to borrow our entire savings. Why not, he says. Burn it all. Eight months later, I buy a one-way ticket to this place.

∞

This new place is made of nothing but distances. It takes hours to walk the entire shoreline, months to figure out the neighborhoods, a whole year to recover from last year's winter. Everyone asks, but no one cares, where I'm from. I meet people from the old country, wonder which language should we speak with each other. David emails from time to time, says that things are getting worse. Father and V send short, handwritten letters in which all bad news have been censored; hers I can read. Luckily, lab rats are abundant and my thesis progresses well. I'm even sent to Germany for a semester, to learn how to dissect rodent brains and stick the tiny soft pieces with electrodes. One sunny afternoon by the Rhine, I borrow a bike to tour the countryside. The night catches me on the way back, as I enter a small forest in which every leaf, mere minutes ago, was ablaze in the setting sun. The darkness is sudden and unyielding. Here and there, the light from my dynamo torch hits the eyes of small nocturnal beasts. I realize that anything could happen, including my complete dissolution into nothingness, without anyone taking notice. The thought is strangely comforting, much like the waves of fresh sweat that keep the evening chill away from my skin. When I return home (my new home), I think often of the Rhineland. The lab rats, however, are endlessly abundant and no thoughts—of Rhineland, homeland, any land— disturb me anymore. In this new place, girls are abundant, too.

I better talk to her, I say to myself, proud of that little pun on the movie title. She was in front of me in the ticket line and now sits one row above, flanked by a girlfriend on each side. That is definitely not my style, approaching girls like that, rushes through my mind, and I swiftly chase away that thought, all thoughts. I keep checking on her throughout the show, but may have stayed silent and motionless had the story been less painful and uplifting, had there not been scenes of love and despair full of beautiful, tormented bodies, had the two protagonists not exchanged amorous glances in the very final scene. Under the circumstances, however, I can't help turning toward her as the closing credits start to roll, my eyes moist with daring and emotion, and there she is, returning my gaze. I mouth a silent greeting, wait patiently until she leaves her row, introduce myself. Six weeks later, we're at the Albion Street beach, fighting a gang of fat flies set on a container full of offerings of love (grapes, dates, chunks of watermelon), plotting our near future, me admiring out loud her confidence and her easy ways, her strong legs and a tight abdomen.

David keeps in touch, writes about things back home getting slightly better, now that Đinđić won and became Prime Minister. He also reunited with his parents. A refugee relief organization located them in a tiny Dalmatian village, almost mad with sorrow. A word had reached them that David got captured in Vukovar and sent to one of those makeshift camps that no one survived. Only when he managed to visit did they truly believe he was alive. After a few days spent together, however, they pleaded that he go immediately and far, far away. It's not worth it, they said. None of this is worth your life. Back in Belgrade, he learned that Hana met a nice British journalist who had reported from every war zone on Earth. And she's not the only one leaving the country, he writes. I received a scholarship, I'm coming to New Orleans.

What does she see in me, I sometimes ask myself. Does she really want to get married and have children? I decapitate rats for a living. I'm prone to feelings of worthlessness, my mood depends on barometric fluctuations. Does she truly expect to meet Father? Now that V's dead (yes, V's dead) and the beach is ruined, can I ever show her who I was? I don't like being dragged to parties full of smart people. I like even less being left alone. Is it love or suicide if I feel like dying when we're not together? Will this gravy of lust and best intentions that keeps us trapped like shortsighted bees congeal with time, and how will it taste then? And what in the world does one do with a degree in Liberal Arts? She introduced me to all her friends. Should I introduce her to David? Will it be mere weeks before he fucks her on the floor while I watch from the couch, faking sleep? And why have I lost desire to chase other women? And what, what about Kumiko? Have I given up on her? Did I not come here to find her? Didn't she say once that she lived in Chicago? I bet she lied. Does Kate lie? She's so irritatingly honest. Her pussy smells like honey. Should I tell her I call her honey because of that?

∞

I like going distances. I prefer walking to driving, train tracks to air travel. I drove to New Orleans once already, caught fire and brimstone preachers on AM radio and a folk song about being one thousand miles from your home. There are cotton fields on the way, giant unclaimed crucifixes, discount factories selling Bibles. I can't not visit my best friend now that he's so close; even Kate says so. I'm so eager to leave all this cold behind, at least for a while.

I arrive refreshed from an unexpected eight-hour sleep in a motel just south of Memphis. It's hot down here already, with the cyan skies blaring with all their might. Every sensation that reaches eyes and nostrils creates enhanced versions of reality. (The nearby lumps of horse dung will grow legs and crawl into sewers.) Even with sunglasses left behind, I recognize David crossing Jackson Square. He hasn't changed much, didn't even catch any tan. We embrace like old friends, but I do worry what will happen when the silence sets in. He doesn't mention Hana, I don't ask. He talks a lot about the city and the new orchestra, about feeling liberated now that his parents are safe; dirt-poor and safe, he adds. He's supposed to stay about a year, but his real goal is Chicago; there's a great, great orchestra there. How wonderful, I reply.

He takes me to his place on Prytania, a small sublet room plus bathroom. I recognize his old cello on the stand, but the casing is new, white and immaculate. He already found a few gigs, he says. That very night he's playing in a joint called Circle Bar, but we should drive around a bit first. And we do. The windows are rolled down and the fragrant air is blasting through the car. Leafless branches of magnolias are heavy with their bubbles of white and purple. My armpits are getting moist with first sweat in months, then dried immediately in the fresh wind. Neither David nor I feel like talking. We drive down Magazine, St Charles, Elysian Fields. We park by the art museum and stroll through the sculpture garden, where shiny silver humanmonkeys are playing in the shadow of an enormous spider. For lunch, we stop at a place named after some French painter and order baked snails, a first for both of us. All this time, Kate is braving sleet in Chicago. Should we move down here as soon as David heads north?

Lightheaded and wine-buzzed, we get back to his place, right on time to take showers and get ready for his gig. David's more muscular than before. His dark attire and raven hair make an intense contrast with his pale skin and the white cello casing. Circle Bar is a few blocks away. It's almost 9 p.m., and the patrons, mostly student crowd, have taken all the good seats. I sit at the bar and watch David as he steps up on a small podium. By the time he's adjusted the note stand, the instrument, his lanky body, all murmur has died out. Good evening, he says, and a few enthusiasts of manners greet him back. Without an announcement, he starts playing "'Round Midnight," then a few more jazz standards. No one says a word; a few people have even closed their eyes. Without a break, he goes through a few pieces by Rachmaninoff and Schubert, then does the Sarabande from Bach's second. According to the great Rostropovich, he says before they've had a chance to catch their breaths, this last one was for those who've known sadness. A rapturous applause breaks out; I see girls approaching, pushing napkins with phone numbers into his pockets. He thanks them politely, every one of them, then advances to the bar. We each have a beer and go back to his place.

We haven't made it through the door and his hand is under my T-shirt. By that time, my mind is made up. I press myself against him and thrust my tongue into his. He grabs me by the waist and rolls down my pants. We rush to the bed and make love in the darkness, the best we can, by an open window, with an owl hooting nearby.

As soon as David is asleep, I get up, get dressed, and affix a note (I'm sorry, we'll talk) to his bathroom mirror. I leave without a sound, except for a brief, subdued cough of the waking engine. The air is still pleasant, so I keep the windows down until I reach the interstate. My body is still content and my mind is abuzz with disjointed thoughts. I don't know what to do, I don't know what to do, I keep repeating, sometimes out loud. I turn on the radio, catch the last verses of a Bob Dylan song, can't remember which one. I never particularly understood Bob Dylan. I reach the motel in Memphis within a few hours, decide to get a few hours of sleep. It should all be clearer in the morning: whom to call, in which order, what to say. The air around Memphis is not too cold either. Tomorrow, I shouldn't forget to keep my winter jacket close. The receptionist recognizes me, gives me the room I had before. It's the one with the view, she says. Only when I get there do I understand what she meant. The dawn is breaking, and the balcony has an unobstructed eastern exposure. I step outside and sit on a plastic chair, hugging knees into my chest. The horizon is opening like lover's mouth, like fresh wounds on the wrists, like a crescendo of fuckedupness. To tame my mind, I turn on the radio. The local public station announces BBC World News. Today in Belgrade, a man's voice says, a tragedy took place. Prime Minister Đinđić, who had narrowly escaped an attempt on his life a few weeks ago, was assassinated as he was entering a government building. He was killed by a sniper bullet that passed through his heart. A state of emergency has been declared.

Truth cannot be found by dissecting heartache, nor does it lie in folds of the flesh. I'm never the first one to fall asleep. I decapitate rats for a living. I do.

MANNHEIM

The Rhine is the color of chestnuts, the color of November. Mornings have been foggy for a while. Anja's living room is aglow with red emanating from the TV screen. A female voice proclaims that plastination will change forever the way anatomy is taught; it will transform our perception of the human body. It was about time, says Adam and pours us each one more shot of some Swedish liqueur, which tastes like bubblegum and smells like dentists' offices. Somewhere with those last words—*unsere Wahrnehmung des menschlichen Körpers*—Professor von Hagens cloaks himself in a white lab coat, in a move sweeping and theatrical, as if fully aware that the director will pick that exact moment for a slow motion finale, zooming in on the professor's irrepressible gaze. In spite of the liqueur, it's clear that we're watching something out of the ordinary.

The bodies—human, animal—are not cut into pieces and forced into glass jars, nor do they exude the grayness of formaldehyde preparations. Even through the filter of a TV screen, one can appreciate their splendor, foreign even to a surgical table: longitudinal section through a woman in her third trimester, longitudinal section through her fetus; a pirouetting ballerina, with her leg muscles—*soleus, gastrocnemius, quadriceps femoris*—spread apart as if on an inverted double umbrella; a man's limp hide hanging over his outstretched arm, his thighs pressed against a horse frozen in a giddy half-motion. The exhibits are in Mannheim till the end of the month; there is a several-hour-long wait for the tickets.

Anja admits that her plan is imperfect, yet simple. Adam, in his Rhineland village, will get up soon after midnight and drive down to Mainz, where he'll pick us up and we'll all go to Mannheim. And what about Andreas, I ask, my tongue faltering, as I point at her swollen breasts. We'll need to take him with us, she says. Markus won't be back before the third, and I simply have to see this.

Anja and I are neighbors, which facilitates the logistics. I knock on her door with caution, but she flings it open in full gear, with an engorged bag over her shoulder, a folded stroller in one hand, and a car seat with a baby in it in the other. At four in the morning, Adam's car is already blinking under the greenish, streetlight-tinted Gutenberg statue. The air, chilly and damp, washes any remaining drowsiness off our faces. Luckily, Andreas seems not to mind the cold, or the heat inside the miniature Opel, or Adam's many attempts to wrestle the stroller into the trunk. Finally we leave, munching on sandwiches from Anja's super-bag. *Komisch*, says Adam with his mouth full, but corpses actually scare me witless. A good enough reason, I say to myself, to invest practically my last pfennig in the ticket.

Adam insists that we converse; he's afraid that he might fall asleep, that we'll end up in ZDF's morning program. Here, look! a purple-faced, matronly housewife would exclaim, pointing at the wet ground, traces of tires, and the car, stuck in between shattered metal arches, as if in the fractured rib cage of some fossilized monster. The noise was horrible! Un-bear-able! Neighbors on the other side of the road woke up! she'd add, while her portly, unshaven husband would join in, struggling for words: New...brand new...greenhouse. Today's youth is so...irresponsible. Anja giggles through a half-whisper, says, C'mon guys, talk about something else—I may have to fall asleep if you continue like that. Adam then informs us that he purchased yet another history book, asks that I tell once more of the war back home. I, however, do not take the bait, and invoke instead my sun-blasted Balkan homeland, invoke the brilliant Chicago October, and let it be known for the thousandth time that—thank God—I won't be staying long. Oh, calm down, protests

Adam, pointing at the frigid darkness. Just look at all these vineyards! They wouldn't be there without sunlight, would they? For about ten minutes there's no retreat or surrender (South against North; *vranac* versus *Dornfelder*), until Anja, her words disfigured by a yawn, pronounces that Adam and I are like an old couple, who, strangely, just met. Then we talk just about anything, slurp from our juice boxes, stare at the void outside. It seems as if Anja fell asleep, too. You simply have no idea of the South, I start again, *sotto voce*. You haven't even been to Majorca—what kind of a German are you? Who in their right mind would go to Lapland for camping? Who nowadays has a herbarium? And with the Baltic seaweed, no less! Adam shrugs, plays his strongest card: *Aber Miloš, das Leben in Deutschland ist gut. Jungs*, says Anja from the depths of the back seat, please be quiet. You'll wake up Andreas. It's not even five o'clock yet.

The plateau in front of the museum is almost packed with cars; the ticket line snakes three times around the building and once more around the parking lot. The plan—to take a spot in the queue and change shifts every twenty minutes—becomes a barely tolerable endeavor: my German is rudimentary, the people around me don't feel like talking anyway, and the moist pre-dawn chill finds its way under my collar with an unnerving ease. After the third shift, the starless night starts fading into a diffuse, slippery morning. Adam duly shows up for his turn, but the reserves of enthusiasm have been depleted. We get back to the car, exhausted, wet with droplets that seem not to have fallen, but chased each other erratically through a fog that looks as if it had been rising from the ground. In the back seat, a ruby-red-cheeked child is suckling in his meal; sweetish odors of a full diaper start permeating the air. No plastination, right? says Anja, still under the cloud of slumber, surrendered to our response. We decide to find some nice place for breakfast.

You've got to admit, says Adam, chewing diligently, that over there, wherever you're from, fast food just isn't this tasty. I have nothing to counter with, finishing my second smoked salmon sandwich, reaching for the calamari fritti with my free hand—all that plus Coke for only twelve German marks. It hurts that the North has won this battle, that a chance to get immersed into preserved tissues and organs is gone forever, that Anja is disappointed (in me too, I know it), but the crowd was forbidding, and the hunger was real. Besides, the breakfast won't render me entirely penniless, which lifts my spirits a little. As if guessing my mood, the clouds above a small circular junction across the street open up a bit, and if not for the soggy carpet of wine-yellow leaves, one would think for a moment that the spring has arrived. Andreas is drooling, chasing a large pendant across Anja's warm, freckled bosom, while Adam attempts to figure out, out loud, who the oxidized mustachioed *Herr* might be, propped up stiff at the center of the roundabout. The dead are "in" these days in Mannheim, says Anja, pointing at a woman with a face lost in wrinkles, who slogs through the heaps of leaves and halts beneath the bust, as if in front of a long-lost acquaintance. A pair of desiccated hands emerge out of her coat pockets; bread crumb flakes start snowing down from her imperfect, arthritic fists. In an instant, a sea of pigeons washes against the pedestal. What she's been collecting for weeks, the pigeons will shit out all over the monument in about an hour, says Anja, bursting with laughter; I burst, too, expressing a few droplets of Coke through my nostrils.

Adam fights with the stroller once again, not quite understanding how he managed to fit it in the first time. It doesn't matter, says Anja. Just put it in the front. Miloš can sit back here, with the two of us. Andreas is deep in his seat, hypnotized by the boob. The clouds seem to have retreated completely: one can make out the blue of the sky through the fog that still pushes down on the hills along the Rhine.

Our road feels improbably tortuous; the fog has condensed into a grayish milky vapor; it's almost impossible to see where we're headed. I hope it doesn't rain again, I say to myself, because a cluster of thunder claps seems to be drawing nearer. The noise, however, does not come from above: right by the car, a scarlet-red horse emerges out of an impenetrable background, then another. An inky breath is gushing out of their rhomboid nostrils;

their eyes are yellow, manes shaven off, bodies relieved of their skin. Their mighty hearts—as if visible: through the muscles, ribs, connective tissue—keep pumping the hot, viscous liquid into their massive flexing quarters; pounding hoofs shoot up handfuls of black, heavy earth. The car gains speed, and so do the horses. The road keeps winding through the hills wrapped in fog; it's a miracle we haven't crashed already. The windshield then ignites with a diffuse reddish sheen, which swiftly solidifies into a sight of a dozen or so human bodies, lined up across the asphalt. A death row, passes through my mind; prisoners, abandoned by their firing squad. The men and women stand radiant, motionless: their eyes lidless, their muscles, blood vessels thoroughly exposed. Right before running them over, full speed, I feel Professor von Hagen's scalpel piercing my left palm; my left jugular, unprompted, starts leaking its contents. The bones begin to snap, crushed by hoofs, tires.

The tires are rolling on the gravel. I hear Adam (*Verdammt! Verflucht!*), the squealing of the brakes. Seatbelts lock up, cutting short our forward motion; stroller wheels smash against the windshield. Andreas wakes up screaming. Slightly panicked— *Was ist los? Was ist los?* —Anja resurfaces from her sleep. Pressure marks from her nails are fading from my palm; on my neck, I sense the evanescent warmth of her drool.

Stranded in front of some barn (one can hear muffled mooing and bleating), we manage to reenter the fog before anyone notices our intrusion. Adam speaks first, admits not to remember the last couple of kilometers. We take a short break. Andreas is cooing, the stroller once more fits into the trunk. In a manner befitting a seasoned Lapland camper, Adam produces a map and a compass. We figure out that the main road can't be far away. We make it to Mainz within an hour or so; I can't recall anymore what we were talking about.

∞

Shortly after our trip to Mannheim, I'll board a plane home. In the beginning, we'll exchange emails almost daily, and then, with memories becoming increasingly demanding, just a greeting here and there. For months to come, the cold will keep peeling sleepiness off my face and paralyze my fingertips; only occasionally, to trick the winter, I'll try to imagine the warmth of Anja's saliva on my neck. Inevitably, with the first nice days, I'll let myself be lured back to life by the treacherous, intoxicating spring, then plunge into the glorious Chicago summer. One weekend, I'll visit New Orleans and weep in shame in the back seat of a cab, with a driver from Bosnia recounting, in his back-broken English, how he narrowly escaped the slaughter in Žepa. I'll send Anja and Adam a postcard each: the Mississippi, the carnival, a never-ending bridge. The very same fall, I'll start taking German lessons, endure them for a full year and a half. Adam and Markus will send cautiously optimistic news, about Anja feeling better, about an imminent double mastectomy. At her specific request, I'll send her a DVD featuring Professor von Hagens's Chicago exhibits; one Saturday afternoon I'll give her a call, tell tales of how I'm doing. Soon afterward Adam will show up, for a conference. As we're getting ready for a night out, a message from Markus will ring in: *Anja ist tot*. That night, Adam and I will get wasted like never before. In the morning we'll take turns vomiting, I'll take him to the airport. I'll return after that to my somber abode, steeped in aromas of bubble gum and nausea. Anja, I'll say softly, or just think it, who knows. I'll sink into a heavy, featureless sleep.

AMERICAN SFUMATO

Miloš's head is buzzing as he keeps thinking, or murmuring, who knows, something about air-conditioned rooms without windows; then about the neon lamps, brains, rats, and the tang of chemicals. After that: the hippocampi and the sea horses, the sea and the horses, cold war, cold sandwiches, cold fingers, hot palms, steamy thighs, the winter, the summer. Once more, for sure, he ponders the rats. Then, for a while, only the frost bites.

How did I get here, how the hell did I get here, laments Miloš under his breath, as a swarm of icicles gathers on his scarf and as his eyes start adjusting to darkness. Came by night, leaving by night, he keeps saying to himself, and then almost shouts: fuck this cold, I just can't get used to it, can't get used to the fucking fifteen below (Celsius) or five above (Fahrenheit), can't get used to the fucking

Fahrenheit scale. Then his mental screen flickers once more with images of the windowless room, third door from the left, at the Biochemistry Department: the one he just abandoned, with a feeling of a massive, thorny crystal forming in his stomach. And it's only been a couple of weeks since he phoned back home: I did it, I became an Assistant Professor! Father was in Crmnica, paying his dues at the Wine and Bleak Festival, or in his case, The Festival of Wine & Wine. Fish is for the pussy cats, I need somethin' that kicks ass, he roared, intoxicated, through the long-distance connection. I need somethin' that kicks aaaaasss, echoed the choir of his drinking buddies; hey, ya motherfuckers, did ya hear that: Miloš has become a professa!

After twenty minutes or so of braving the ice and the freezing wind, during which he masterfully managed—not once, but three times—to avoid an abrupt encounter of his nose, bottom, back with the petrified snow, Miloš finally reaches the three-floor apartment building that has been his residence since the past July. On the facade, only two windows are illuminated: in one he can make out Kate, already in her new coat, staring into a frigid, streetlight-suffused darkness; the other is visited by Camille, briefly, but long enough for Miloš to realize that she opted for a miniskirt in this bitching cold weather. I'm late, I'm going to be late, how the hell did I get into this, he grumbles to himself, unwrapping the scarf, sprinting up a few flights of stairs.

Hey hon, you late, you late, and you know it's not Halloween, says Kate in her broken Serbian, pressing her warm cheek and lips to the general area of his face, anesthetized with cold, and then moves on, direction bathroom, carrying a grinning, bare-bottomed child over her shoulder. Hi, Mr. Milosh, says Camille, passing by equally fast, but without a kiss, alas, without a kiss, holding an equally grinning child, and you know, she adds, it's a good look for you, and releases her curt, almost shrill giggle. Miloš then makes a step toward a mirror, where he meets a puzzled, pale, half-frozen creature, someone who looks like him, for sure, but otherwise a strange fellow, someone who put on his puffed-up down jacket over a blood-stained lab coat, which makes him look quite unconventional, like a ragged clown on the verge of tears (I'd say), or even a resident of some restricted-access institution, one of the more reliable sort, someone who handled his drug regimen well and was allowed to take public transportation home for the weekend. Miloš's cheeks are still burning with cold, and his brain feels a little numb, too, which is why he can't even blush, or come up with some witty or meaningful reason for choosing such attire. It's very sad, he thinks, that the first thing that comes to mind is a scatterbrained-scientist cliché, sad indeed, because that's the cliché he despises above all others, as he gets rid of the jacket, since he hasn't, no, he has never been scatterbrained, or even distracted, crumbling up his lab coat and jamming it into his backpack, it's only

that he's overworked, because, he zips up the
backpack, for years now he goes to work by night and
returns by night, and thinks hey, idiot, you're gonna
be late, as he conjures with anger, with bouts of
disgust, the image of himself in that accidental
costume of his, a costume, he starts to believe, that
gives him away so mercilessly, as only costumes are
capable of doing.

Then he too heads for the bathroom, where Kate is
about to finish her brief makeup routine, and where
Camille, kneeling by the bath tub, oversees Sasha
and Sophie in their bubble bath universe. It's easy to
make fun of the working class, tries Miloš as easy-
goingly as he can and grabs his toothbrush, the tip of
which, he never fails to recall as he switches it on,
can reach up to thirty thousand super-brief jerks per
minute. *I know you're glad to see us, hon*, protests
Kate, again in broken Serbian, *but you know we have
two bathroom*, upon which Miloš shrugs and grins
with his mouth full of foam, which, stirred up by the
turbo-speedy bristles, sprays everywhere around,
especially over an arm of Kate's new coat. Kate
releases a theatrical growl, because she only rarely
loses her cool, and leaves the bathroom in haste,
upon which Miloš locks his lips tight and lowers his
gaze to Camille, whose perfect, muscular legs now
lie folded underneath her red-green tartan skirt. She
looks at him coyly, like an accomplice, like someone
who's having lots of fun, and he has serious trouble
keeping his eyes on hers, the color of ripe

blackberries, because just a chin below opens up a path into the depths of her radiating bosom, across which his children have already cast luminescent handfuls of the bathing bubbles.

Have fun, you guys, and don't worry about them, chirps Camille in her happy soprano, while Miloš and Kate, withdrawing to the door, apply exploding kisses to the twins' enormous cheeks. At the sight of their parents disappearing, the children release *mamadadaaa* in unison and start advancing across the living room. Camille has to react fast, because Sasha and Sophie, as she knows too well, ignore the fact that they started walking only a month ago, and hurl themselves and stumble and run into furniture edges with their soft temples and foreheads. In the bustle that ensues, Miloš manages to anchor one thorough look into the depths of Camille's inviting cleavage, and maybe he would have stayed that way had Kate not pulled at his arm and said, c'mon, let's go already.

In the frozen seats of their car, adjusting their minds to silence, fearing that they'll hear screams of brain-injured children, Miloš and Kate manage to exchange their first intimate glances of the day. Our first date in six months, says Kate and turns the key, waking up the engine of their white Honda Civic. And she also says: *if we're late for the movie, honey, I swear, I kill you.* Miloš is sick of the cold, of almost solidified breath that's leaving his nostrils, and says sorry, it was a complete madness at work, Dmitri and Ken were exchanging their childhood stories, so they missed their turn for the ultracentrifuge, but see, we're on time, we're so lucky that we've found Camille. *Hon, if you don't stop talk about lab, I also kill you,* replies Kate, looking at him askance, smiling with the corners of her mouth, and moving her index finger, in lieu of a knife, across her muscular, elongated neck.

Miloš welcomes the fact that Kate decided to drive: he hopes to be able to focus, to round up his thoughts, to redirect them, no, to blow them away by some unexpected cortical winds, to expel them everywhere, without mercy, actually to stop thinking at all, neon lamps, windowless rooms, to halt the pestilent brain, let Dmitri and Ken now have their fun in the centrifuge room until three in the morning, let them compare their childhood stories all they want, a suburb of Saint Louis and the very downtown of Dniepropetrovsk; luckily, one can at least count on Wei-Chen, he's the only one who has no desire to recollect sad and funny tales of his childhood, although, truth be told, he did tell him once about the long-gone days, about his father the colonel and growing up in the garrisons, about the frozen steppe by the Mongolian border and the holes in the ground for the prisoners of war. As Miloš tries to rein himself in, Kate examines herself for a moment in the rearview mirror and, before shifting into drive, takes off her gloves, rubs her palms against each other with considerable fervor, and presses them, almost ignited, to Miloš's hurting earlobes.

The Honda already feels like a small Japanese oven, the heat suffocates Miloš's cerebral storms, and he finds it harder and harder to spin the thoughts of rats, hippocampi, American-Ukranian friendship, and Chinese-Mongolian deserts. Kate also senses that the turbulences in his head are winding down, and her thin and forceful fingers, endowed with an impeccable timing—something that, it has to be said, Miloš always appreciated greatly—abandon the stick shift for a second and clasp themselves around Miloš's unsuspecting quadriceps. Hon, don't sleep, she says, *I'm so curious, email says that Todd Haynes will come maybe, he once was in our college, and it was great.*

How to handle the latest Todd Haynes movie? *Far From Heaven*, he recalls, was unbearable; he simply can't get the Americans' obsession with the fifties, as far as he's concerned the most boring decade in the history of decades. As if reading his thoughts, Kate says you may actually like this one, and with a short, vague announcement (for which one can be grateful), puts in a CD that Miloš can't make out in the darkness, nor does he hear what else Kate has to say, since the car has reached the shoreline curve of Sheridan Road. It's pitch dark and the lake is invisible, but Miloš knows it's there, omnipresent, with its lid of thick ice and snow, the anti-Adriatic, fish-infested steppe, a sight that always left him breathless. Then there's a guitar, the murmur of the crowd, the nasal voice of a young man in his very famous song; then the applause.

The Honda Tropic rushes down Lake Shore Drive; the night is cloudless and still, only a stray car here and there, Chicago's North Side on their right, and on their left the enormous lake, stiff with cold. Kate's mood improves by the minute, she says I know you'll have fun, Cate Blanchett's in it, and so's Charlotte Gainsbourg, but Miloš has checked out for a while, his forehead pressed against the window, sleighed far into the lake, the anti-Adriatic, maybe the Adriatic Sea itself. Kate places her hand on Miloš's thigh one more time, and, after fifteen or so minutes filled mostly with small, unrelated words, the two of them sail onto the rooftop of a garage. The sudden silence of the extinguished engine startles them both, interrupting Kate's inner musings about the movie, Miloš, and the passage of time, as well as Miloš's fantasies involving large bodies of water, and for a second or two the car is devoid of a single word or thought, until someone says, it's not exactly clear who, I can't believe it, honey, our first date in six months. Then they leave the vehicle—which has already started succumbing to the cold—examine the surroundings as if checking for surveillance, and then, hand in hand, enter a shopping-mall-slash-movie-theater.

Judging by the crowd around the cash registers, there are quite a few people anxious to see Todd in person. Miloš frowns, suppressing the ever stronger need to grumble, but Kate, who loses her cool very rarely indeed, reaches into her coat and takes out two pre-purchased tickets: the wonderful, reliable Kate, so unwilling to allow overcrowded cash registers to spoil anything. Hey, look over there, it's Amy and Pete, she exclaims, pointing at a couple waiting for the tickets, upon which Miloš says great, I'll be right back, I need to get one, you know I have to. I know, shame on you, she says, *prior vegetarian; I want one too, with many mustard.*

Carrying them both in one hand, two inviting, foot-long hot dogs, adorned with rich applications of mustard squeezed out of an oversized plastic trough with a pump, and holding, in his other hand, a huge styrofoam cup full of sparkling diet Coke—almost an entire liter: the portion that he and Kate go through when in the movies, fighting for the same thick straw—Miloš manages to maintain his balance through the crowd and locate his wife. It's still not quite clear, he learns, whether Mr. Haynes is going to show up; he also learns that Amy too remembers his visit to the Modern Culture and Media Department at Brown. For some inexplicable reason, Miloš is convinced that Todd will stand them up, but he keeps that uncomfortable thought to himself, feeling just fine, listening to a very musical duelling of smarts between Amy and his wife, bringing the lukewarm hotdog to his mouth, exchanging a glance or two with Pete, who also did not go to an Ivy

League school, and then says Pete, my fwiend, sowwy, thif hot dog isfo good, did you watch Fav From Heaven, how did you wike it, and Pete says no, I didn't. Then it's Pete's turn to say something: Miloš is chewing, listening politely, no, he on the other hand did not see that one, and then, noticing that people are slowly flocking in, wraps one arm under Kate's—while holding, in the other, with a great deal of effort, the bottom of the enormous cup and his partly finished hot dog—and starts pleading that they enter before all the good seats are taken.

We apologize, but Mr. Haynes won't be able to greet you this evening, says a young man, stepping bravely in front of the audience and asking for silence, which forms only briefly and then dissolves into a faint sigh of disappointment, followed by a reluctant applause when Mr. Haynes's latest movie finally begins. Miloš can't say that he really understands what it is about, other than Bob Dylan, incarnated by several men and the divine Cate Blanchett, and that's okay, he thinks, since he kinda always liked his music, but above all the lyrics: catenating images, troubadouring rhymes, women, history, social injustice, then women again. There he is, a black boy who's Bob Dylan, riding a freight car through some America. He's surrounded by hobos, bad intentions are on their faces, like when they take away his guitar case, on which it says THIS MACHINE KILLS FASCISTS. Those exact words were on Guthrie's guitar, says Kate in her softest cinema whisper, and the boy jumps out of the train to save his dear life, life of a fascist-killer, and plunges into an icy, greenish river, where he's swallowed by a great white whale.

An hour or so into the movie, diet Coke finds its way through Miloš's system and he needs to leave his seat for a moment. As he urinates, it seems, three or four minutes at least, with a feeling of doing it in a Todd Haynes' bathroom, he realizes that he'll have to admit to Kate, because fair is fair, that this movie is quite compelling. Then, as he rushes back to his seat, men's and women's rooms open simultaneously (Miloš swears that's how it happened), and he almost collides with a dark-haired woman wearing a short black dress. Miloš's eyes skip over her features (Asian, petite, beauty mark at the tip of her left eyebrow), and his heart leaps and his diaphragm starts trembling, pulling along the entire abdomen. Excuse me, she says, passing him by, leaving a vanishing cloud of fragrance in her wake, which makes Miloš's innards go absolutely crazy, and he pulls at her arm and asks, Kumiko, is that you?

I beg your pardon, says the pretty Asian, I'm sorry, he retorts clumsily, don't you remember me, it's Milosh, from Kotor, nineteen-ninety-four. She smiles, she wears a lot of makeup, maybe it's not Kumiko after all, because this girl readily says, sorry, it must've been someone else. Have you ever been in Kotor, Montenegro, Adriatic coast, he goes on, stubbornly, but she just shakes her head, that must've been someone else, repeats, and glides back into darkness.

Sorry, it's all that Coke, Miloš says to Kate, taking her warm and bony hand, as Cate Blanchett Dylan rolls down some English lawns with the Fab Four. Aided by the greenish reflections from the screen, Miloš manages to locate a female silhouette devoid of sharp features, three rows in front of him, and he's dead certain that it's her.

It was the summer of ninety-four, almost the climax of Yugoslav wars, and that's something that Miloš doesn't like to talk about, something he even hasn't told Kate, who at the time was deep in subjects that were taught at Brown University's Department for Modern Culture and Media, passing her days without a slightest notion that there was a Miloš, who was spending that summer, like most others, in his aunt's house for rent in the coastal town of Kotor. During winter, the aunt was a florist and a state oil company employee on permanent furlough; during summer, she rented rooms of her semi-dilapidated villa to whomever and for whatever price, because the times were ugly, and no one had any money, and there was happiness with no end when some Americans showed up and said that they needed room and board.

Miloš can't recall exactly what it was that they were doing in Kotor, those Americans, each one occupying a room in The Flower, the town's foremost bed and breakfast. He remembers that it had to do with the war, peace, understanding among peoples, but also that none of that mattered at all, since the situation was developing beyond all expectations: already on day three, he was sniffing fresh sweat from the nape of her neck, while the indolent air from the bay was breezing in slowly, and the sun was taking its time to emerge above the steep mountains, as if reluctant to shine on the world in which everything, finally, was as it should be. On day five, he rented a boat and they went to Perast, where they pressed their bodies together on the mosaic floor of a roofless sixteenth century palace, while on day six they took to the open sea, so that Kumiko could set foot on that wondrous beach, which, ages ago, before there was tap water and asphalt road, was rumored to be the only pristine cove on the Adriatic coast. Alas, they were chased away, by men with thick skulls, black guns, and fat racing boats, so they returned to auntie's *pensione* and made love with fortitude and sadness, until the sun came up one more time, until they both collapsed with exhaustion.

In the early afternoon of the seventh day, while Miloš was procuring food for The Flower, the Americans packed up their stuff and vanished: without an announcement, forwarding address, or farewell letter. Auntie just shrugged, went once more with her index finger over a tiny roll of US dollars, and shuffled away to clean the emptied rooms. Miloš searched everywhere he could: along the coast, in Podgorica, even Belgrade, and then decided to follow his father's example and drown himself in wine & wine. He was not his father, though: by next summer he sobered up, shaved off his freshly grown bohemian beard, and managed to enroll in a Neuroscience PhD program in Chicago. He knew her name, body, and the complex topology of her scents, and that he needs to do his absolute best to find her.

The years that went by turned Kumiko into a queasy memory, one to which, we can only assume, Miloš occasionally masturbates with sadness. Women, and everything else he yearned for, marched through his life in a sufficient quantity, so when one day he saw Kate, standing in line for the latest movie by Pedro Almodóvar, he could finally be sure that what was driving him was not hunger, or despair, or the pointless need to forget (what? and whom?), but the pursuit of happiness, so precious and so simple. Had he succeeded in tracking down Kumiko, he was sure, it would have ended very badly, just as badly as it now ends between Charlotte Gainsbourg and Bob Dylan, played on this occasion by Heath Ledger.

The real Dylan finally appears, blowing a solo in his most famous song; the closing credits roll, Sonic Youth start singing I'm not there, I'm gone. Kate stretches in her seat, enthralled, with her eyes moist, with the exact same look Miloš saw after the manly Marco and the beautiful Alicia—in the fateful Almodóvar movie—exchanged glances at the end of a show in which everyone, Marco and Alicia, Miloš and Kate, would be awakened from the domesticated horrors of their everyday existence by a ballet piece with a happy finale. The audience leave their seats, a few enthusiasts clap, careless feet trample over crumpled popcorn bags. Miloš can't resist and looks around, but the Japanese girl with a lot of makeup is nowhere to be found. Sure it's better this way, a thought zaps through his head, and he too shakes hands with Pete and Amy and says goodbye guys, it was great to see you.

At the garage rooftop, while scanning their surroundings (because a night like this, in which hands are held atop an immense, winter-riddled city, is almost mystical and deserving of special attention), Miloš grabs Kate around the waist, draws her near, and nails his manly smooch on her grinning mouth. Happy birthday, he says, and produces out of nowhere a tiny faux-mahogany box. What's this, asks Kate, who likes surprises after all, but Miloš stays mum and lets the moment unfold, in which Kate lifts the lid of the heavy little box and discovers a pair of tar-black trilobites, curled up in obedient repose, conjoined with the light-gray limestone in which they were fossilized, and at least, this Miloš says out loud, at least five hundred million years old. Kate's laughter bursts among the rooftops, and that's how this story could end.

The story, however, does not end that way. We know for certain that, after Kate's petite happiness explosion, the two of them got into their white Honda Civic, turned up the heat, and put in the I'm Not There soundtrack, purchased immediately after the movie. At about the same moment the car reached the empty Lake Shore Drive, Jim James & Calexico began their moaning version of "Goin' to Acapulco," Kate, with her lips tightly pressed together, released a stream of silent tears on the collar of her new coat, and Miloš, yet again, went sailing the vast memory expanses. After she parked in front of the apartment, Kate asked out loud, in a voice tamed and upbeat, whether Sasha and Sophie are asleep, and Miloš, we can be pretty sure, seized a moment to conjure an image of Camille, of her warm bosom and her deep-dark eyes. At the end of that very long day, chances are that Kate and Miloš fell asleep in each other's arms, with their limbs tangled up and glistening with sweat, like a couple of trilobites that copulate readily and swiftly, as if sensing the limestone boulder, a bed of chalk in which they'll remain curled up for the next five hundred million years.

Hey, Mr. Tambourine Man, won't you please emerge, come for once out of your troubadouring fog, screw visions, women, and social injustice, and please, please, play a ballad just for me. Play me of the days that hang like drops of honey, of ten-fingered fists of heartbroken lovers, of longing that blows up windbags of one's chest, of giggles and tears and bones and best intentions. Then make a mention of the rugged clown (of me, as I am, as I'm writing this), wrapped up in russets, mottle and moth-bitten, of yearning that makes his skin sore and scarlet, of pathetic gifts for which he is ready (Dylan, Brown, concert—all the best, my dear), weariness of silence, weariness to talk, weariness to scrape away this powdered chalk.

RATTUS

The memory fails me; the images pressed into my softness are entering oblivion like the contours of a beach that's being abandoned in haste. (The patter of the engine; the sobs of a pubescent girl in a polka dot bikini; a towel sprouting thorns, some of them crimson red; the foamy, spreading wake; the silent, bare-breasted woman; the gathering darkness.) If you take the hippocampus (by way of decapitating a *Rattus norvegicus* pup, *exempli gratia*), slice it like a banana, and stain it using the procedure of Franz Nissl, each slice will offer a sight of curved dark purple regions that resemble a horn, traversed by long fibrous tracks. If an electrode is planted into the tracks that stem from *Cornu Ammonis 3* (the region named after Amun, who rose above Mantu the falcon and became the sun, the creator, and the ram) and lead all the way—all the few dozen micrometers—to

Cornu Ammonis 1, and if the said electrode is then used to give the fibrous filaments two distinctive, identical jolts, say, thirty minutes apart, then another electrode, planted in the *Cornu Ammonis 1* region, will register a stronger response to the second jolt. The theory of cellular memory formation holds the first stimulus to be analogous to the original event: the crowd gathers in a square below a church, praised be the Lord and his steady, vengeful hand; the beach is now sliced up with zigzagging concrete walkways, occasionally covered with goat droppings; the house is in flames; all but an aquarelle of dubious commercial value is lost. The second, augmented response is considered to be a consolidated reaction to the original stimulus. *Memoria, id est; memoria in statu nascendi.*

The memory fails me. But I do recall them coming in waves, burrowing themselves underneath my finger nails and marching up my arm, dissolving into the bloodstream as they reach the shoulder. To make things worse, my left thigh is compressed by a trapdoor that leads into the hold of this steam-propelled contraption that patrols the frozen Mississippi. Or it could be trapped underneath any of the multitude of objects that litter the deck: folds of hot, heavy, heaving human flesh; grids of hot steel that stir up the aromas of fresh sweat and dried bodily juices; a turned-over motorcycle, its wheels spinning, abuzz with echoes of a well-known ballad (yes, but which one?); slabs of limestone, bubbling with petrified trilobite remains. Underneath the ice, the dense, opalescent liquid is inhabited with giant whales, paintings that bleed color, human bodies (flayed, discarded), underwater lamps that turn on and off like the eyes of silent movie actors. Although everything around me appears frozen (the water, the skies, the moss-covered trees by the river), the ship glides undisturbed into the horizon, dragging me along, emanating heat that makes my chest exude translucent plums of sweat. My face occasionally scrapes the ice; at those moments, the urge to do something, to save myself, overwhelms me.

The objects on the deck reshuffle (first with hesitation, as if weighing their options), and then, in a single, seemingly coordinated move, release my leg from its stolid bind. That frees me up to turn on my side and pull out my infested arm. The minuscule creatures halt and scurry back, pushed by my blood reclaiming its vessels. Kate lifts her head, just enough to let me readjust, and her fingers, warm, firm, warm, pass over my chest and abdomen to my crotch. The steam vessel assumes the shape of Kate's mighty hips, the frozen river dries into labyrinthine folds of our bed sheets, and I start to sense the full presence of her naked body, glued to mine by the sticky leftovers of love.

Sitting on the bed, I wait for the rebellion in my temples to subside; I need all my strength, all of my resolve to stand up, move to the window, and quiet the radiator possessed by spells of hissing. The outside is still frigid and immobile, with deep snow that turned into pale, dirt-covered rock weeks ago. A few drops of sweat slide down my back, leaving traces of chill in their wake. I wonder what it feels like to be trapped in the inner space of our newly installed windows: one pane covered with blotches of crystals, its twin exposed to vapors generated by primitive heating systems (residential steam pipes, human bodies).

I stand above Kate for a while, watch her lie squarely on her back, with limbs bent as if stopped mid-stretch. I then hover with my nose over her dark pubis, which makes my mind swirl with the aromas of raw meat and honey. Some of her hairs are up, some sleeked against the skin, and some have detached from their roots and strayed up to the pale tissue ridge that marks the spot at which the twins were pulled out. They let me hold her hand and watch it: the metal utensils and the expansion of the opening; the extraction, the first cries, the cutting of the cords; the sewing up of her shrinking uterus, her iodine-smeared belly a makeshift working surface. Kate turns on her side, shoving her knee into my face. What are you doing down there, hon, she asks, then falls back to sleep.

I peek into the kids' room and see them both curled up underneath an electric yellow moon. I tiptoe to the bathroom without turning the light on, mount the toilet, and release a stream of urine that sounds like a testimonial, a confession that ends with a few flourishes of sobbing. I wash my face, armpits, and the genitals, find clean underwear and a T-shirt in the belly of the dryer, grab a blanket and move to the couch. The disarray of toys dominates the living room even in the darkness; I need to mention that to Camille. I then picture her on all fours, in her tight blouse and a tartan mini-skirt, as she picks up the items, one by one, and puts them where they belong. A flicker of erection passes through my penis; I seize on it, bring myself to a quick hurrah, deposit my semen into a fresh tissue, and adjust my position against the cushions and the backrest. Once again, I congratulate myself for resisting Kate's idea that we save fifty dollars a month by canceling our subscription to premium cable.

I pick a channel that usually shows a comedy I've seen a dozen times already. Instead of the opening scene, however, there's a red-headed man smiling at me, his compressed cheeks apparently eroded by a massive acne invasion. The letters on the screen reveal one M.F. BUSTLEY, MD, the founder and chief officer (operative, medical, executive, financial) of LIPOFAITH CLINIC & SPA, in the year nineteen-eighty-two. I don't feel like reaching for the remote. This movie must be really boring; it will put me to sleep faster than any comedy. But the man doesn't wear a shiny bluish suit anymore, nor is he seated in a shiny faux-leather armchair. He now shifts nervously in a plastic white seat, clad in bright orange, occasionally drumming with his fingertips on a simple desk. His ginger curls are visibly thinner, a microphone button is attached to his collar. How did you become a plastic surgeon? an off-screen voice asks—a Pentecostal preacher, a person involved in the Balkan politics on the highest level, a yacht owner, an investor, a convicted tax evader? Can I start from the beginning? Please do.

I was born Milivoy Frederick Bustley, says the red-haired man; San Fernando Valley, California, nineteen-fifty-two. In the school, the kids who liked to tease me called me Millie; the few others called me Freddie or, on occasions, Bus. My father was an insurance salesman. Mother had a hair salon, among the best in the Valley. Your father: What was he like? I don't remember much of him; he was rarely there. And mother? (Silence.) Anything else about the parents? How did they meet? Were they from the Valley themselves? Could we stop the interview, please? Are you sure? Yes.

I'm sorry, I've never been interviewed before. No problem; why don't we continue? Okay. Are your parents still alive? Father—I guess not, but who knows? Mother died twenty years ago. About the time you went to Africa? Yes. She died senile, in a nursing home. As you know, I couldn't really visit. I'm sorry you didn't have a chance to say goodbye. Thank you.

What's your favorite memory of her? The way she was putting on her makeup—as if dressing up for a battle. Morning after morning, I'd watch her do it and think: beauty is much more than our features betray. She took her time with each step, sometimes accentuating the eyes, sometimes her high cheeks or her lips. Sometimes I'd be late for school, because I couldn't stop observing that ritual. You excelled at school, right? I'm not ashamed to say that I was the best. I always knew how to apply myself. Who else was good? Only Nancy Villanova came close. Who is she? (Silence. Close-up of M. F. Bustley's face with his eyes closed. The effect appears staged.)

Back to your father... There's really not that much to say. He was rarely there, busy selling insurance. Busy Bustley, they called him. He'd even introduce himself that way. He was in LA all the time, staying late, leaving early, seeing us on weekends only. Then one Friday night, a few days after my tenth birthday, he didn't come home. We thought he got injured in a car crash, or worse; called the police even. Then on Sunday morning a guy came, talked to my mother at the doorstep, gave her a package, and drove away. What was in the package? Ten thousand dollars. Who was the man? I can only guess. What's your most reasonable assumption? He and my father performed an insurance scam together; the man got his payment, split it with my father, and came to give us our "share." (He makes air quotes, barely lifting fingers from the desk.) That is, whatever father thought we should get, after he was safe and away in Brazil, together with his masseuse. You assume that your father ran away to Brazil with his masseuse? I pretty much grew up believing that. Why? That's what the guy told my mother. It made sense. Your father left no note? Never called? Never.

Could you tell me more about the girl you mentioned, Nancy Villanova? Yes. Her father was a cardiologist from Mexico City, married to a daughter of an American consul. He had a thriving private practice in the Valley. My mother did Nancy's mother's hair. Nancy's mother was astonishingly beautiful; the only one who comes close is her daughter. Were you friends in school? We were okay, but never close. I was smitten by her since the first day we met, but out of her league—in almost every way. Is that why you went into medicine: to impress Nancy? It seems like it now, doesn't it? It didn't back then. What did it seem like?

I did it for the beauty. Now, like then, I believe in two things, strongly and irrevocably: Beauty and the God Almighty. In fact, if you let it, the former can lead you to the latter. How did you pay for the medical school? The ten thousand dollars helped; I also got a scholarship. Father never sent any more money? Never. What was Nancy doing? Studying medicine as well. The same school? Yes, UCLA. Did she specialize in anything? Pediatrics. Did you try to get close to her on the campus? She would barely acknowledge my existence. I thought it was my face. I was miserable, lonelier than ever. What happened next? I applied myself. Again, I was the best in class.

Again better than Nancy? Oh, yes. She had way too much of a social life. Did you have any? With those hippies? Not really. But everything happens for a reason: had I been more outgoing, I wouldn't have had my epiphany. Of what kind? I accepted Jesus Christ as my Lord and savior. I got baptized by the Holy Spirit. Where was that? In a Pentecostal church, downtown LA. Which one? Does it matter?

Did you speak in tongues at your baptism? They burst out of me like water through the mouth of a thirsty hose. What other manifestations of a spiritual awakening did you experience? I heard my name pounding in my head: Milivoy, Milivoy! Then I saw myself holding a scalpel and this heavenly creature that very much resembled my mother descended from the roof. She invited me to caress her skin with the blade, and wherever I opened it, a beautiful flower grew. See, God was presenting me with a calling. To become a plastic surgeon? Yes! The scalpel, the embodied beauty, the flower—how much clearer can a message get?

After the baptism, my surgical skills improved formidably—as if my hands were divinely guided. (He looks at his hands.) Even now, I sometimes find it easier to do simple procedures, like the stitches, with my eyes closed. My professors swore they had never seen anything like that. My fellow residents were full of awe, and even fuller of envy. As a result, the little social life I had collapsed completely. But with God, you're never alone.

Your name: who gave it to you? I was named after the paternal grandfathers of my parents. One was Frederick T. Bustley, a pharmacist from Detroit, where my grandfather the pharmacist and my father the insurance salesman were also born; the other was Milivoje Jovović, a village priest back in Montenegro. Montenegro, former Yugoslavia? Correct. Your mother was from there? She was born Irina Jovovich, in Detroit as well, but her father came over in the 1920s, to work for Henry Ford. His father, my great-grandfather, was a priest with a sword, who fell in disrepute with the Montenegrin king and was killed by Turks in an attempt to clear his name. Is that what your grandfather told you? I had no chance of remembering him; he died of lung cancer the year after I was born. My mother, however, she was always very proud of that family lore—proud to come from such a lineage. And so were you? Let me ask you: what would you rather be? A descendant of small businessmen and philanderers, or a great-grandson of a black-robed hero who died for his honor? (Fade out.)

(Fade in.) Why Lipofaith Clinic & Spa? I told you: it was my calling. As a young and brilliant plastic surgeon, you could have worked anywhere. I didn't want to work anywhere; I wanted to stay in the Valley, establish myself, and ask for the hand of Nancy Villanova. But you said yourself that she barely acknowledged your existence. Let me ask you again: Are you a believer? I beg your pardon? Do you believe? You mean, in God? Anything! Do you believe in anything? Humanity, I guess; our ability to search for meaning in a critical way—but not much beyond that. And I was awash in the mercy of our Lord, inundated with the Holy Spirit many times, and witnessed great spiritual thirst, great potential, great vision in people you'd probably call delusional or criminal or worse! And they were full to the brim with love for God, and so I know His word must be true! And He showed me the way. And I didn't waver. Not until much later.

So you came back home a hot plastic surgeon. Your mother must have had one of those rare parental moments in which pride, sense of relief, and yes, vindication, come together. She did, at first. But she began deteriorating soon afterwards. In what way? It could have been the Alzheimer's, or a series of mini strokes, no one knew for sure. Shortly after I came back and opened the clinic, the first signs of illness appeared. Within a year, the salon needed to be sold. Not long after that, I hired a live-in nurse. Mother withdrew to herself, kind of realized what was coming. But that didn't deter you from expanding your operations? Well, there was still a life to be lived, and my calling to answer, and someone also needed to pay for the nurse. How did you get the idea for the clinic and the church, operating simultaneously? A less devout person would call it self-evident; for me, it was all part of the plan. I was meant to spread the gospel of Beauty, both physical and spiritual.

Couldn't it all have been mere greed? You mean me perpetrating fraud, like my father? I'll forgive you such preposterousness. I never felt like I was defrauding anything or anyone. I lead prayers with all my heart, and prayed fervently for all of my patients. And visions, glorious, intricate messages from God would descend upon me regularly, leading my hand, giving me inspiration for manipulations of the skin, the fat, the cartilage: techniques never before seen in medicine. As I told them at the trial: my faith teaches that healing cannot be received without prayer; I came to believe that it can't be given without one either. Yes, but churches are exempt from certain taxations, and for-profit enterprises—like your clinic—aren't, as you must have known. In *IRS v. Bustley*, the judge drew heavily from an expert evaluation by certain Raul Ivan Gomez, an IRS agent specializing in tax evasion. As documented by Agent Gomez, you represented the Lipofaith Clinic & Spa's income as contributions made by the congregation of the Church of Divine Intervention, which was, conveniently, founded and run by you, in the same building where the Clinic & Spa operated. I don't see your point. Many of my patients were my congregants as well. It was only natural that many were baptized by the Holy Spirit under the same roof their features were touched by the power of the Almighty. For me, there is no separation between the inner and the outer sanctum. Once the Holy Spirit races through your tissues and fills them with Lord's mercy, there's no distinction anymore between the center and the periphery; periphery is central.

But that's not the ground on which you and your lawyer tried to dispute Agent Gomez's report? Of course not. His assessment was not borne out of due diligence demanded by his profession or even sheer ignorance of the tenets of Pentecostal faith; it was an act of betrayal, vengeance, and pure malice.

Please explain.

Remember the photo you said you'll use for the movie? This one? Yes. (The camera zooms on the grinning visage of a young man in a shiny bluish suite. The close-up is dominated by the flash flooding the craters on his face, something he tried to prevent with massively applied makeup.) We've also discovered that same photo in the archive footage of a local TV station that ran a story about your case. Yes, I remember that well. They played that "in-depth profile" (diminutive air quotes again) during the trial; cost me most of my patients. They zoomed on my face at least three or four times, augmenting the effect of the acne. But what is it about the photo that's so incriminating in regard to Agent Gomez? The station got it from him personally. How do you know? Because Nancy took that photo, with my own camera, and only two prints were ever made: the one that mother kept on her night stand and the one I gave Nancy as a gift. Agent Gomez insists that it was Nancy's idea, but I'm sure he manipulated her or took it against her will.

So you and Nancy... I should feel like a fool, shouldn't I? But I don't regret it. So you did manage to establish a relationship with her? She returned to the Valley shortly after I opened Lipofaith, opened a pediatric practice of her own. Her father used to host this annual event for local medical practitioners, and I made such a name for myself, I couldn't be ignored anymore. So I finally passed through the white lacquered door of their house, with my mother under my arm. It was the last happy memory for the two of us. Nancy's father even mentioned me and my clinic in his toast, something to the effect of his daughter being such a brilliant young physician, and by the way, someone else from her class succeeded as well. I found a quiet place in a corner for mother and myself, but people kept approaching us, asking about prices at the clinic, scheduling appointments, chatting with mother about the latest haircare trends. To my surprise, she handled the conversation well. At one moment, Nancy came and pulled me aside. I'm sorry, she said. I was wrong to ignore you all these years, especially at UCLA. I wanted to enjoy my freedom, and nothing to remind me of my home. I saw a glimmer of well-tended sadness in her face, realized that it couldn't be perfected. I asked her out for a lunch. She said yes.

What happened then? Over the next year or so, we kept seeing each other every couple of weeks. Each time it'd be a little less awkward than the time before. She mentioned no suitors, I believed she had none. The invitation for the next annual party at the Villanovas' place came not from her father but from Nancy directly. Unfortunately, by that time mother could not go out in public any more. When I showed up, carrying a bouquet of white roses, Nancy and her mother simultaneously smothered me with hugs. Pressed between so much beauty, drunk with the scents of roses, the women's perfumes, their olive epidermises, I nearly collapsed in exaltation. When I stepped into the backyard, it was already full of people, some of them my patients and congregants. The moment he saw me, Nancy's father introduced me to a "family friend," a young guy who smiled a lot, said that he'd heard of me, admired me greatly, asked questions about the Pentecostals, the church, the clinic. We drank a lot. Nancy looked at me a few times across the party, and all I could see in her eyes was admiration. (M. F. Bustley's eyes appear to fog with suppressed lacrimation. The effect appears genuine.) Accepted into the family circle, I thought.

And then? I was trying to see Nancy more often, even asked her out for a dinner once. She was still kind to me, but somehow more reserved. I thought she too was realizing how serious the situation between us was becoming. I began bringing her flowers regularly, each time a new kind. Then one day my assistant at the clinic tells me that Agent Gomez from the IRS is there to see me. I step outside and face the young man Nancy's father introduced me to. Raul, I said, is that you? Hi, Fred, he said. Would you mind if I asked you a few questions? No worries, he said, pure formality.

I found out about their engagement during the trial. My attorney tried to invalidate his testimony and report as personally motivated, but the judge laughed him out of the office. I think Nancy's father was pulling the strings all along. But the Gomez report itself was audited, right? One IRS agent checking the work of another—you can't be serious. Didn't you pay that other agent, who was not employed by the IRS at the time? That was my stupid lawyer's idea. However, I had other priorities. Like what? Like seeing Nancy. I wanted to ask for her hand; the one thing I always wanted to do. But she stopped answering my calls, and my letters would return unopened. What else happened during the trial? My business suffered; congregation, too. Mother turned silent, more and more withdrawn, with occasional outbursts of rage. I understood what needed to be done. And what was that?

As soon as Agent Gomez left my office, I started moving along shady areas of my life, those that even I barely knew existed. I acted instinctively and with premeditation at the same time. I fired the nurse and placed mother in a nursing home. I sold our house and arranged that her stay be paid for as long she lives. The day I took her there was the last time we saw each other. (I wish I embraced her longer, says M. F. Bustley, turning suddenly to me. I wish she reeked less of imperfect hygiene, of old age; I wish her makeup wasn't so thick, so chaotic, so misapplied. Do you understand me, Miloš?)

I was maintaining the appearance of business as usual and, by the time Agent Gomez's testimony was made, already managed to move most of my assets abroad. I paid the penalty for closing the lease too early on the clinic and the church, and had to sell the house for half of its market value to the first person who was ready to pay in cash, but those were pretty much the biggest hits I took. On the very day I was scheduled to be crucified by the jury for doing God's work, I crossed the Mexican border. Within a few weeks, I was in Brazil.

Brazil? Yes. I went to Salvador da Bahia. I had already purchased a small apartment there, under an assumed name. I lay low for a while, then used my cash reserves to procure a Brazilian passport and medical credentials to go with my new identity. Why Brazil? Well, it had nothing to do with my father, if that's what you're asking. For a plastic surgeon, there's only one place in the world as good as the US; in some respects, even better. I got a hint of that a few years prior to arriving: I had showcased Lipofaith at a conference, met some surgeons from Rio, heard tales of Ivo Pitanguy and his breakthroughs. And not to forget: through my fellow

Pentecostals, I'd heard how strong our denomination in Brazil was becoming. And why Salvador? I was worried the IRS and the FBI would send my name to the Interpol; as you know, I wasn't totally mistaken there. I thought I'd be much more exposed in Rio, the center of my craft. You leave impression of someone who carefully plans his every move. If that were the case, my friend, would I be sitting where I'm sitting? (M. F. Bustley sends me a small wink. I wonder why it took him so long to acknowledge me again.)

Doctor Ignacio Montenegro keeps to himself for the first year or two. He spends very little time in the Salvador apartment he purchased as M. F. Bustley, alias F. T. Job, alias T. L. Lukich, via several intermediaries. Instead, he settles in Chapada Diamantina, deep in the Bahia countryside, in a decrepit village hut that cost him close to nothing. There, he introduces himself as Dr. Frederick Job, an American who fell in love with many splendors of the region and decided to spend the rest of his life there. He applies himself as only few are able to and soon begins speaking like a local; he even starts performing all the duties of a local physician— everything but childbirth. Dense ginger curls spread across his face, like keratinous ivy; to his quiet delight, he notices that the lesions on his skin are no longer visible. In his free time he hikes the area, rests on treetops, sleeps in caverns or in a small military tent, given to him by one of the villagers in gratitude for closing up a foot wound that wasn't healing for years.

Not long afterward, he acquires another piece of cheap property, on the very coast, where a wooden hut is soon erected, which he names *O Paraíso*. He spends a month or two there each year, sitting on an empty beach, staring at the Atlantic, fantasizing about sharing those moments with a good, faithful, fruit-bearing woman, an embodiment of beauty, someone sublime and refined, with a name as seductive and filled with promises of bliss as Nancy Villanova's. After nearly three years in the wilderness, Dr. Ignacio Montenegro returns to his small apartment in Salvador and realizes with elation that the neighborhood he had chosen in haste is full of social climbers and actually perfect for a small clinic dedicated to personal improvement, which he then purchases from a local practitioner of *plàstica* who was approaching retirement.

Thanks to the reasonable prices, modernization efforts advertised in the local press, and a masterful (some would even say divinely guided) touch of the new, mysterious, bearded surgeon from Chapada Diamantina, the clinic *Beleza Eterna* becomes a local phenomenon. For the most part, Doctor Montenegro keeps to himself, but the rumors have it that one of his ancestors was a Slavic hero priest slain by the Turks in the nineteenth century, and another a sailor on *The Beagle* who got off the ship in Salvador, in the time when the ship's most famous passenger (of whom Dr. Montenegro doesn't think much, he makes that much clear) wrote the following: "For the first time in my life I saw the sun at noon to the North... I am constantly surprised at not finding the heat more intense than it is; when at sea & with a gentle breeze blowing one does not even wish for colder weather. I am sure I have frequently been more oppressed by a hot summer's day in England."

Within a few years, Dr. Montenegro becomes the most sought after *plàstica* expert in Bahia. His reputation begins to swell and spread like a surf wave, and invitations to join professional associations, both local and national, and attend conferences and workshops, start flooding his mailbox. Such popularity fills him with both pride and unrest, and he cannot find peace even among the fellow Pentecostals, whose ecstatic tongues sound nearly identical to those heard in the churches of the Valley or LA, places he now recalls only vaguely. He is also somewhat disturbed by the fact that he's not visited by visions any more, but by men in dark suits passing by the clinic, day or night. And his mother's voice is distant and unfocused: he can practically see her sitting on the other side of the line, staring at the courtyard pines, mumbling some slobbery syllabi to her black-robed caregiver. (Sister Janice is always kind to Dr. Frederick Job, Mrs. Bustley's cousin from Detroit. She admires him for calling long distance so often, especially since Mrs. Bustley's own son seems to have forgotten his mother completely.) Once more, Dr. Montenegro shifts to the survival mode, like a rodent that keeps to himself, to the shaded areas of life that he now understands a little better.

To shake the men in dark suits off his tail, Dr. Montenegro registers for the annual meeting of Brazilian Breast Augmenters and Reducers, announces his week-long absence from the clinic, and purchases an airplane ticket to Rio and back. A few days later, in the window seat of a plane that approaches not Rio but Belém, a thousand miles in the opposite direction, he cannot help but smile. He may be doing it in wonder, at the sight of the mighty Amazon delta below, but more likely he just thinks of the faces of people in dark suits, as they examine the contents of a piece of luggage in the restroom of an airport restaurant. He pictures them rushing in, guns aloft, wondering what could possibly take a man so long, and then discovering in one of the stalls a deep purple suitcase they've been keeping in their sight all morning. He practically sees them ripping it open and then realizing that it's empty, save for the familiar Hawaiian shirt, a pair of khaki trousers, and handful after handful of prickly, freshly cut ginger curls.

In the port of Belém, Dr. Montenegro mails several pages of typewritten instructions to his assistant surgeon in Salvador, advising him to burn them after reading. He is confident that his junior colleague will do as asked, because the proposed deal would benefit them both, especially the young doctor, ambitious and of humble means. He then boards a nondescript freight vessel bound for Cape Town, South Africa. At the open sea, he cautiously congratulates himself for outrunning the pestilent human law yet again and spends the few clear nights staring at the starry splendor above. The remainder of the four-week trip he finds himself barricaded in the officers' common room, a move forced by one raging storm after another. In the bluish haze of tobacco smoke and alcohol vapors he meets Vojin, a radio operator who, when inebriated, can't stop babbling about (a) his prostitute girlfriend in Hamburg, Germany, (b) his home country, by the name of Yugoslavia, where, unless there's a massive interference in radio signals, the civil war is about to break out, and (c) names: of academics, apparatchiks, bank executives, bishops, dentists, former dissidents, generals, literature professors, police chiefs, poets (at least a handful), psychiatrists (at least two), warehouse supervisors, writers (several handfuls), zoo managers—all involved in a mass murder scheme that has yet to claim its many victims. In the same haze-filled room, Dr. Montenegro befriends Jeff, a deputy security officer. Despite his voluminous belly and disheveled appearance, Jeff appears to be a true connoisseur of the human form, particularly female. (He recites the differences in size and proportions between the most admirable fashion models, past and present, with ease and astounding precision.) Astonishingly, in addition to their addiction to beauty, Jeff and Dr. Montenegro also happen to share a Montenegrin ancestry, with Jeff actually being somewhat conversant in the language of their forefathers. Dr. Montenegro is intrigued by these coincidences, but even more by the fact that Jeff chose to reveal those details to him and not to Vojin, with whom he could have actually practiced his ancestral tongue. This alerts Dr. Montenegro to a couple of important points, not least among them the fact that Jeff is a bit like him: a person of dedication and intelligence, yet a careful one, someone who surveys his surroundings carefully and is not lead astray by impulses of the moment. Their friendship is sealed one particularly stormy and drunken night, when, on their way to the cabins, Jeff asks the doctor whether he believes in God. He also mentions that his spiritual meanderings keep bringing him to Orthodox Christianity, the faith of the old country, a subject Dr. Montenegro doesn't know much about but agrees is worth looking into. In Cape Town, the passenger and the officer remain on land, united in something better than a plan: a shared vision, a production-worthy script in which they both play stars, a promise of a promised land.

Is that where you met the metropolitan? Some may say we were lucky; I believe we were simply ready. We learned in Cape Town of a Serbian Orthodox church, the only one in South Africa. After a few days, we got there and discovered a humble edifice, its contours vibrating in the sweltering heat. Inside, a bearded, black-robed man was standing in direct sunlight, surrounded by sparkles of dust, immersed in prayer, yet with his eyes open, his forehead devoid of a single drop of sweat. Jeff approached him in his crippled Serbian; he answered back in decent English. We asked for an audience with him. What did you discus? He introduced himself as one of the metropolitans of the Serbian Orthodox Church. We told him that we learned about the unrest in Yugoslavia, and how we decided to return to the land of our forefathers and aid the Serbian cause. With what, he asked. With our experience, our dedication, our business acumen, we answered. I told him about my priest ancestor, which created quite an impression—the legends I was told as a child were apparently true. And Jeff learned from the metropolitan that, judging by his last name, mangled by several decades of English mispronunciation, he must belong to a seashore Montenegrin clan that preserved their Serbian Christian faith through the centuries of Turkish rule. So what happened to your Pentecostalism? The metropolitan and I had a separate meeting about that. He explained it well. Thanks to him, I realized that Orthodox Christianity and Pentecostalism both spring from the same desire to seek pure, undiluted truth. He opened his heart and shared some of his visions with me, which did resemble those that I used to have, before they abandoned me in the narrow alleys of Salvador. I was moved by his humility. I knelt before him and the tongues came to me naturally, ready to burst out, but I took a deep breath, kept my organ in my teeth.

The metropolitan saw my struggle and asked me to repeat after him: *Gospodi pomiluj*. God, have mercy. And I did. The tongues remained inside, twisting themselves into an unspoken, unspeakable word of the Almighty. I learned so much in just one day. And then? Both Jeff and I got baptized the following morning. You changed your name again, correct? I did. After that, everyone knew me as Dr. Ignjat Crnogorac. I don't expect you to be able to pronounce it.

Upon his arrival to the land of his forefathers, Dr. Crnogorac (alias Dr. M. F. Bustley, alias Dr. Frederic T. Job, alias Dr. Ignacio Montenegro, the moniker we shall, mercifully, continue to use) is first quartered in a white monastery built into a side of a mountain. Taking a full day off his busy schedule, the metropolitan takes him to a place not too far away from the monastery, the exact spot where Dr. Montenegro's priest great-grandfather was slain by the Turks. The metropolitan discovered the site himself, he says, following the clues from local decasyllabic folk ballads which are told by night, when exhausted bodies and thirsty spirits gather around the hearth, and when a village bard, aided by a single-stringed instrument that sounds like a wounded ox, wails the verses about heroes and their heroic demises. The metropolitan sits down on the cold earth in the middle of a vast naked field, asks that the single-stringed instrument be fetched from a shiny black Mitsubishi Pajero SUV parked nearby, and renders the story of Dr. Montenegro's great-grandfather's rise and fall with virtuosic bravado. Everyone present—Dr. Montenegro, Jeff, the bodyguards, a young deacon—feels the morning chill spread to their shaken, unworthy cores.

Following the metropolitan's recommendations, the two new arrivals remain sequestered among the young, curious monks until they mastered the Cyrillic alphabet and became reasonably fluent in Serbian. Upon leaving their shelter, in the summer of nineteen-ninety-one, their ways part briefly. Jeff travels by foot to the seaside (which takes him a full day and a half), to the land of his ancestral clan. With metropolitan's blessings, he befriends important people fast, starts a private security company, purchases a house by a bay, and, soon afterward, a boat. Dr. Montenegro takes a different route: he boards a small government plane that occasionally takes the metropolitan to his important missions home and abroad. In Belgrade, the capital of Serbia, Dr. Montenegro experiences for the first time the power of connections working for, and not against him: within a few weeks, he meets with several academics, apparatchiks, and bishops, plus a dentist, two former dissidents, three generals, one literature professor, two police chiefs, a handful of poets, two psychiatrists (one of them a poet as well), a dozen writers, and a zoo manager, and is promised a meeting with a warehouse supervisor too. Everyone finds his life story downright inspiring (the episode of tricking the hydra of the American legal system twice especially working in his favor), his black robes are taken as indisputable evidence of his dedication to the Serbian cause, and a few academics make a convincing case that his ginger curls constitute a definite proof of his Slavic origin and identity. Your Serbian soul is screaming through your skin, says the metropolitan at one point, commenting on Dr. Montenegro's pale complexion and red hair, which brings Dr. Montenegro to the epiphany that the soul-to-skin transmission of features is the most profound law of the nature, not the babblings of that ridiculous passenger of *The Beagle*.

In January nineteen-ninety-two, Dr. Montenegro places his first long-distance call in months to a nursing home in California, during which Dr. Frederic T. Job learns that his cousin, Mrs. Irina Bustley, passed away in her sleep a few weeks prior and that she has been interred in the facility's cemetery according to the Orthodox ritual, as requested in the enrollment documents, for which an Armenian priest from Sacramento needed to be summoned. The same month marks the end of the metropolitan's direct mentorship over Dr. Montenegro. On January sixth, the eve of Orthodox Christmas, in the capital of Montenegro (still called Titograd, but not for much longer), the metropolitan and his protégé are at the foot of a hill, in a churchyard that overlooks a square full of people who chant in ecstasy and carry long flags, which, seen through Dr. Montenegro's eyes, resemble eels caught in a net. (The flags are mostly red, blue, and white, with a cross in the middle and an outward facing C-shape in each of its four corners, but there's an occasional Jolly Roger, too, in good mood as usual, encircled by slogans in Cyrillic.) Tall dark cypresses, planted in a row perpendicular to the wall that supports the churchyard's plateau, separate the square from an abandoned cemetery. A platoon of men wearing camouflage uniforms and red berets stand between two men in black robes and the church. At the metropolitan's silent sign, the platoon members aim their AK-47s in the air and fire three short bursts into the night clouds. The crowd falls silent; the flags slink down their poles. The metropolitan steps up to the microphone, invokes a Merry Christmas in the ancient Slavic dialect spoken in church ceremonies only. The songs and cries explode again, louder than ever. Dr. Montenegro isn't entirely sure, but he seems to discern verses that invite feasting on the blood of infidels. What intensely pious folk, he thinks. He also seems to notice a face in the crowd that doesn't really belong there, that of a young man who kind of faints but has no room to fall. The movement of the crowd takes the man away from Dr. Montenegro's sight. I hope he doesn't need a doctor, he thinks.

I hope you didn't need a doctor, Miloš, says M. F. Bustley, shifting nervously in his plastic chair. I try to respond, but every time I open my mouth, an elastic membrane forms between my lips and absorbs my every word. That prompts M. F. Bustley to stand up, walk past the interviewer frozen in an interrogatory pose, and press his eyes against the lens of the camera. Fascinating structure, he says; it even has its own blood supply. Wondering what he means, I open my mouth as wide as I can, which makes the veins on the membrane bulge and turn dark green. I can touch them, trace their branches, sense my own pulse when I squeeze them between my tongue and fingertips.

So you opened your plastic surgery clinic in Belgrade in nineteen-ninety-two? Yes, in March. Was it difficult? Are you kidding? In those days, it took at least a month to collect the twenty-five requisite pieces of paperwork to open a hamburger joint. I had all of my paperwork done in a single afternoon. Where did you get the money? My savings, of course, harbored safely in a few Swiss accounts. In addition, *Beleza eterna* was doing very well back in Salvador; my former assistant did what I asked of him and was wiring me my share regularly. Who were your clients? The usual: the nouveau riche, the politicians' wives, the diplomatic core. I'd also fix up a disfigured soldier here and there. And what about the rumors that you helped two war crime suspects change their appearance and performed extensive liposuction on the president's wife? I can't comment on any individual case. I took an oath that I shall protect my patients' privacy. Was there anything that was asked from you, in exchange for such an easy access to resources and prestige? Nothing that I wouldn't have provided willingly. For example? I can't say more. How long has the Belgrade clinic been in operation? For ten years. I closed it in early two-thousand-two, soon after my old friends were swept from power by Đinđić and his street thugs. The ascent to power of Dr. Zoran Đinđić, who, as you know, was assassinated in the year two-thousand-three, is widely recognized as a key event in modernization of the Serbian society. Please don't lecture me about things you don't understand. Have you seen the metropolitan again? Several times: the last time when he asked me to go to the States on a mission that could potentially reverse the political fortunes in Serbia. What kind of mission? I'm afraid I'm going to have to keep that a secret as well. At any rate, and as I'm sure you know, the mission is not the reason I'm here.

It is early morning in the summer of two-thousand-two when Dr. Montenegro knocks on the white lacquered door of Jeff's seaside house. The two men embrace at the doorstep like two long-lost comrades, then take a seat on the terrace that overlooks the quiet bay. Dr. Montenegro explains that their common cause will require him to take a trip to the United States in the near future and that, considering the fact that he still may be wanted by the FBI, additional efforts need to be made to keep his American identity under wraps. Together, they concoct a plan they ultimately deem not inferior to the one forged in the underbelly of a Cape Town-bound freight vessel. As Jeff elaborates the outline, with Dr. Montenegro nodding in careful agreement, a young red-haired girl, the neighbors' daughter, passes by the wrought iron fence and waves them a good morning.

Soon thereafter, I. Montenegro Enterprises Ltd is established in the coastal municipality of Budva, and a cocktail party is organized in Jeff's house to honor the occasion. An assorted group of academics, bank executives, consultants, government officials, poets and writers, police high-ups and generals, politicians, professional dissidents, public relations specialists, theater directors, and entertainers is invited, and speeches are given that celebrate the natural wonders of the region, economic patriotism, and the entrepreneurial spirit that will attract many high-spending tourists. In his toast, Jeff explains that his good friend, Dr. Ignacio Montenegro, whose forefathers emigrated to Brazil from these very shores in the early twentieth century, will helm the enterprise, and that he already made his first big investment: the purchase of a brand new yacht that is going to be delivered any day now, and which will be named *Nancy the Beautiful*, in memory of Dr. Montenegro's recently deceased mother. As the party heats up, Jeff cannot but congratulate himself for putting the entire deal together, and also for adding his neighbors' daughter to the list of his employees. He can't take his eyes off her as she moves through the throngs of guests with ease, carrying trays with snacks and refreshments, deftly evading sticky hands of men and equally sticky gazes of women. What a beauty, thinks Dr. Montenegro, his eyes fixated on the same spectacular sight. What a piece of work, except for that oversized nose.

The three of them disembark on the beach from a small motorized vessel. What did I tell you, says the girl, isn't it perfect? My father told me that, long time ago, before the tourists and the yachts, this was the most pristine beach on the Adriatic coast. But will it accommodate a yacht, says one of the men. Of course it will, says the girl. You will make it happen. A few columns of smoke rise above the surrounding trees and shrub, and both men already know that the hands that set those fires in the stoves are knotty and wrinkled. Their children are gone and will not return, but they can find them. They can offer a fair compensation and proceed with building a paradise. A vision flickers in one of the men's mind, that of a long beach bar, with bottles shining aquamarine and gold in the morning sun, and a simple name, almost forgotten. *O Paraíso*, thinks the man; oh, how sweet a memory. The man also envisions his own initials, engraved in the planks of a small beach hut.

Fascinating, Miloš, fascinating, he keeps repeating, his eyes still glued to the lens of the camera. He cannot avert his gaze from the throbbing membrane spread between my lips. I still try to utter the words that I've been saving for him for so long, the questions I burned to ask, but in vain. Two hands emerge from the background and drag him back to the white plastic chair. Look at me, the interviewer says; look at me, Mr. Bustley. We need to carry on. Please tell me: how did you get caught in the end?

The yacht sails away. The once-festive crowd is now silent, concerned about the mood of their mysterious host. He promised further investments, says one of them aloud. What if this incident makes him change his mind? The bar that he personally designed, the marina that he built, all those houses that he purchased and planned to redevelop—the entire project tarnished by this unfortunate event. In his dark cabin, the host thinks about the schmuck who spoiled his biggest party yet, who was caught stealing artwork and then left bleeding on the beach. Through a pair of binoculars, he observes a diminishing dark figure prostrated on the gravel and another one that emerges from the bushes. It must be the girl that disappeared, the man thinks, then turns his binoculars to the thick dark cloud that keeps growing above the beach. Another girl, a red-haired beauty with a bloody nose and dark bruises under her eyes, wraps her arms around his shoulders and tells him not to worry: she'll make sure that the little asshole and his girlfriend both get punished for what they did. What a savage that little punk, the man thinks. He almost broke her nose, a mere week after he had fixed it so well. Who told him we were there? And why did he go for those paintings in the first place, in a cabin full of much more valuable items? I told that idiot who reeked of cheap liquor, thinks the man with the binoculars, I told him I won't touch the house as long as his mother lives. I know what it feels like to have an ailing mother. Who did these paintings, I asked. Take them, the guy said, all but this aquarelle. But I like that one the most, thought the man; I may be able to get it later. He must have hired the little schmuck, thinks the man with binoculars, to steal them back from me. Well, my friend, there's a fire now, consuming your precious old home. I hope your mother feels better, you ungrateful vermin. Luckily, the man thinks, the time of his mission is coming. He could use a break from all this madness.

So they picked you up at the O'Hare Airport? Immediately after landing? Yes. Apparently, there's no escaping the police state these days. My fingerprints from all four continents, photos, transcripts of the phone calls I made to the nursing home—all assembled in neat folders on some stupid interconnected servers. It will take a couple of years to get out of here. And once I'm out, I'll have nothing and be nobody once again. Is that why you agreed to participate in this documentary? To have your story told?

You wish. I'm doing this for the children, for those who will come to take our place. I'm doing this in the faint hope that hope still exists, that it hasn't been pulverized, blown to smithereens, spread around for free by the followers of Charles Darwin, by the generic pop divas with vulgar boob jobs and poorly lifted asses, by the revenue service officials. I'm doing this because I still believe in God and his son, Jesus Christ, in Christ's miracles and the power of the divine providence. I'm doing it because I can't accept that my road ends here, in this unworthy dump. I know that God won't let me fail, leave me unable to accomplish my mission. One of these days, you see, Agent Gomez will stop by. I'll observe that the process of aging has consumed him more than me. He'll then tell me that their oldest child—a boy, the first of three, all of them tall and handsome—is ready for college. And so be it. Blessed be the flesh and blood of Nancy Villanova. Because one day I will be out of here, ready for more. You, Miloš, you will never stop floating through your maze of reveries. But this rat will escape his cage undamaged.

RE: NELLIE MCKAY SONNETS

Amy, dearest,

We've just arrived. I can't say I've seen much yet: mostly nondescript soc-realism, not a tree in sight, hot as hell. Miloš assures me that I'll like it better tonight, when he shows me around a bit. We're stuck in a hotel room now, trying to keep ourselves awake for a few more hours. Gotta go, will write more later.

K.

∞

Kate claims that she thought of Amy a lot the night we went out, that it would be right up Amy's alley to see some of the alleys we walked by. She's also aware, she says, that her report may be making this place more visit-worthy than it really is (I disagree), but admits that we did have a good time, a very good time. She's correct in recollecting that jet lag wiped us out for most of the day, and that, for that long at least, we didn't have to endure the humid heat everyone seems to be complaining about. It's obviously important to her to mention that the hotel is new, very American, and right in the middle of everything. In fact, *it's right across the street from Miloš's college building*, she wrote (emphasis mine), and a corner away from an underground restaurant where David and I met for the first time. (Stop giggling, babe, she says; I can practically hear you.) And it's also true that we woke up around five in the afternoon, entangled in sweat-soaked sheets despite the very American air conditioning, our eyeballs aching, and managed to stumble out of the room within an hour. We did eat at the hotel and then went out to examine the area. I don't get the mild sarcasm, for example when she says that I wanted to give her a tour of my tormented youth years. We were simply there, both by accident and design: I did pick the hotel, but she was the one who asked that we cross the small park with green-tinted sculptures of two nineteenth-century men of letters, which brought us right in front of the dark cubic edifice that wafted—Kate couldn't help noticing, no one could—odors of something strange and unpleasant. At that moment, true, I couldn't resist pointing at the windows of the lab where I spent my last few years here, which, she says, made her hungry with curiosity to see it. Also true, I did say that there's no way they'll let us inside, upon which she did sprint up a flight of wide, eroded stairs and knocked on a huge glass door, and the night guard did show up, all sleepy and confused. He actually seemed glad, Kate thinks, that someone came to talk to him on a Saturday evening. I, however, think that he was simply taken by Kate's athletic beauty, and, propelled by the slobbery hardening in his pants, decided to follow a rule by which no ordinance of his employer (University of Belgrade, in this case) could possibly apply to him. Kate doesn't mention that detail, but his enthusiasm was gone the moment he saw me running, much less gracefully, up the same flight of stairs and putting my arm around Kate's slender waist. But the big glass door was ajar, and I did furnish a few details of my previous engagement in the building (making it sound more recent than it really was) and dropped some names, and he did agree to let us in and escort us to the first floor, after taking our passports hostage. (Such are the regulations, he explained. Kate doesn't mention it, but that move got her really unsettled.) The corridors were pitch black, with some machines whirring behind unseen doors, and the scent of chemicals we sensed outside was quickly turning into a definite, oppressive stench. (Think pharmacy with a dead rat under the counter, she explains. Nice one, hon.) The lights in the corridor flickered, and I lead us to a textured glass door that still bore the name of my long-gone mentor. We stepped inside (my old lab, I remember thinking; *Miloš's first lab!* wrote Kate), the guard turned on a few more flickering stripes, and the first thing she claims she noticed was a few machines on the benches, their platforms rocking steadily, carrying plastic trays with pale-blue liquid and some gelatinous material inside. In that same sweep, she also claims to have taken in the obviously outdated furniture and the first item that caught my attention: an ancient turntable on a shelf, tucked in between two blocks of tightly stacked LPs. She writes about me approaching the LP collection and pulling out a Grace Jones album (Amy, dear, don't ask me which one, she says, you know I'm horrible with that stuff), then sliding it back at the exact moment the guard told me not to touch anything. (Hon, if you ever get to read this: the album was *Living My Life*, released in nineteen-eighty-two. "The Apple Stretching," a ballad about New York City mornings that ends the Side A, kept me warm and going on many an intolerable day, back when I was young and tormented.) After that, I tried my luck and did ask the guard if he could also let us into the office attached to the lab, and he did oblige, although already very much annoyed, smirking and posturing and making it clear that we'd pretty much exhausted his supplies of good will. (A good-looking guy, babe, she writes; you'd definitely like him.) We quickly entered the narrow room, most of it occupied by a huge naked desk that, she observes, I could not help laying both of my hands on, *as if needing to retrieve*, she says verbatim, *images, fantasies long-faded*. I don't get this departure from her usual style, so matter-of-factual and no-nonsensical, but she's definitely right: touching the desk (an imperceptible gesture, I hoped) was aimed at connecting with the memory of a few bitter-cold nights spent on that very surface, with Hana, back in the days of youth and torment, with our battered bodies covered with nothing more than my molting down jacket and the sticky leftovers of love. We thanked our escort, collected our passports (to Kate's visible relief), and stepped outside, back into the hot, excessively balmy evening, which was filling up fast with the Saturday night crowd. It's been a while since we went out, she said, and I agree, it was kind of strange to hold hands in public, especially here, with part of me fearing that our amorous routine would spark the flames of jealousy in the heart of a nameless, faceless, long-abandoned love interest lurking in the shadows nearby, all made up and ready for the night out, but suddenly conflicted between pretending not to have seen us and dousing us with her pepper spray. Our palms pressed together, we turned into a dark street that opened into a block or so of tightly packed bars, each enveloped in its own cocoon of obnoxious contemporary pseudo-music. We didn't stop there, however, but kept going downhill, toward the Danube (yes, *the* Danube, I remember saying, wondering for the millionth time how someone with an Ivy League degree could be so oblivious to the basics of European geography), passed by an empty farmers' market that reeked heavily of pot and something rancid, and stopped in front of a church that had been converted to a theater and jazz club ages ago. As we got closer, Kate claims to have caught my smile (I did smile, I guess) before realizing that we'd come to a Nellie McKay concert. She breathed in a loud wow, then paused, and then simply remarked: *Here?* Correct, my love, Nellie and the band were on the program of a local festival, which, I agree, does seem ridiculously improbable. (And yes: surprising you does take effort.) You know, babe, how much I wanted to see her live, she writes. (I know, hon, and now you know why I was so insistent that we didn't postpone our weekend alone, Father's worried face and the kids' adjustment issues be damned. At least he's been sober for a full year. And I do appreciate your not filling Amy in on that matter.)

Hon, I agree about one more thing: the concert did take us back to that winter afternoon years and years ago, in New Orleans, with David asleep in the back seat and a local NPR station on, when we heard Nellie play and sing and answer Terry Gross's questions and were both smitten by how she sounded and what she said, and by the fact that she was only eighteen or nineteen at the time, and I admit to having imagined our threesome, ever so briefly and not too tastefully. And all those years never a good chance to see her live, and all of a sudden here we are, and Nellie's here, too, in an old-fashioned gown with floral and avian motifs (or could those be birds that turn into flowers mid-flight?) and her strong but delicate voice is filling up the massive nave of the church with ease, and your muscular fingers are resting in my palm and I could swear that, in one vanishing instant, my and Nellie's eyes locked and there was this invisible flash of resonance between two beings who have little in common but belong to the same clique of the disillusioned, the exhausted, the hyperactively pessimistic. Of course, I couldn't have shared such frivolities with you, so I suggested instead to not go straight to the hotel after the show but move deep into the narrow alleys that surround the church, well into the muggy darkness, and walk all the way to the Danube. (Yes, *the* Danube.) Last but not least, you report correctly that we were holding hands all the time, that we met very few people on our route along the river, and that it's not really clear who suggested that we play a game of inventing sonnets on the spot, with the only rule being that they have something to do with Nellie or her lyrics. I'm disappointed, of course, that you didn't try to recreate any of them for Amy, because it turns out that I'm forgetting them fast, and you may, too, and by the time you're up the new day will inevitably begin draining our heads of everything that took place tonight. Just like I'm about to drain these pages of any proof of my shameless snooping, lest I forget, just like you did, to send, delete, log out before surrendering to jet lag, and you may get up while I'm asleep, and see all this. I wish I tried remembering our poetry instead. I wonder what else we've neglected to write down, how much of us will stay with us in the morning.

∞

Amy, babe,

Here's the fourth installment of my travel diary. Yup, Belgrade was surprisingly fun, I'm still recovering from Miloš's great Nellie surprise, and kind of trying to figure out how to organize the time now that we're reunited with the kids and Miloš's dad. And in midst of it all, I thought of you again. Remember that Italian movie from the nineties, with a bearded guy on a Vespa, who goes island-hopping with a friend? And remember the island of... I'm blanking on the name (of the island, guy, movie: everything), but I do recall a scene in which they visit a village ruled by children. The parents indulge their precious brats to the extreme, which somehow leads to waking them up at night, no matter the age, to guard them from the unspeakable horrors of "the loneliest hour." And after the twelve-year-old dictator babies have been woken up (sweet revenge!) and moved to the wrought-iron-framed beds of their parents, the reading begins. The parents read aloud, everything, the entire house libraries of the Italian middle class, especially the classics, including Tacitus' complete works. And that's, of course, how you came to mind. Miloš's dad took the kids out for a walk in the 100+ F weather, and they came back with faces painted in all the ice cream colors locally available (yes, Grandpa, too), and the scenes from that movie rolled in front of me. Remember us seeing it together at Brown, mere days after you've had to turn in that forty-page whopper on Tacitus, and us laughing hard, half-drunk and completely stoned, madly happy?

So that's what we've been doing: staying in Miloš's dad's apartment (there's constant bickering between the two about some renovations—past, present, future), waiting for the late afternoon, for the heat to let up a bit, then walking through a park full of massive, perfumed pines, descending a few hundred stairs, and then taking a dip in a green, ice-cold river. All of this in the middle of the city! The kids love it: the water's as cold as Lake Michigan's, but the scenery is more dramatic, and there are plenty of pebbles for stone skipping. Yesterday, we added a twist to this afternoon fun, as Miloš took us to a place where this river meets another (whose bed was nearly dry—that's how hot it is), ten or so miles upstream, where the deepest part of the canyon ends. We were practically alone on the beach, surrounded by willows and blackberry bushes, and the blazing blue sky above us was uninterrupted, save for a dark rectangle of a bridge that we had to cross to get there. The water temperature was even more intimidating, even more in contrast with the dry sweltering heat of the air, a shrinking-expansion stress that, of course, the kids seemed not to mind at all. I figure you find all this more than boring. I'm getting a bit bored, too, and can't wait for the promised week at the seaside. Stay tuned, say hi to Pete.

Love, K.

∞

OK, I didn't delete that thing—just tucked it away in a hidden folder. But I may do it after I'm done with this one. Or the next one. We're both to blame that we came to this trip with just one computer, and yes, it's my fault only that I can't resist snooping on you (knowing you better, really), but yours and only yours that you forget logging out of your email account. I expected to see more of David in here (yes, I know, that's probably why I'm doing this), and I'm relieved not to have found anything that would make me unzip my skin and run around screaming, but I'm still puzzled over a thing or two. For instance, you tell Amy all about beach-going in the city, but keep quiet about what happened yesterday and last night. Why is that? After all, it was your idea to take the kids to the cemetery. They just turned five, you said, it'd help them understand better the phenomenon— or did you say *the concept*?—of death, and it should be relevant from the cultural heritage point of view as well. And you also wanted to visit Mother's and V's resting places, which, honestly, I do admire, even love about you. And that's what I don't understand: you write about pebble skipping on the river and the blackberry bushes, but not a word about Father lamenting about keeping kids away from the graveyards, about us being crazy for risking heat strokes for the entire family. No mention even of the bench at the cemetery, the one under the wall of cypresses where you had to seek shelter from the sun, or of Sasha and Sophie yelling "Dragon water! Dragon water!", pointing at a water tap nearby in form of a dragon's head, and you turning it on, and the water somehow bursting out all over the three of you, fresh, ice-cold water, which evaporated from your clothes and hair and skin within minutes. You also say nothing about the screaming cicadas, the air vibrating above tombstones, the faces in marble that stare back at you from everywhere around (there's your cultural relevance: I don't recall seeing portraits in American cemeteries). Also not a word about the three unlit chapels by the gates, each with a casket surrounded by mourners and the summer flies, or about people in black moving slowly across a small Sanpietrini-paved circle, seeking shadows, secreting sweat instead of tears, wiping it in slow motion off their crumpled faces.

You also don't mention that you disappeared. I of course did notice that you got up, immediately after all the lights were out and Father's snoring from the living room became regular, and then I heard the entrance door opening and closing. It couldn't have been the bathroom door, it has a different click to it, plus there were no sounds of flushing or water tap or anything. Then I got up and yes, your sneakers were gone, too. I did try to be rational about it. Where would you go in the middle of the night, in a city you don't know, in a country whose language you don't speak, without a cellphone that could work here? I went back to bed, determined to give you half an hour before alerting Father that you went missing and going out to find you.

Then I got up again, went to the kids' room, and sat in the chair by the balcony. There was even some breeze coming in, which, together with the sight of kids' faces in the half-darkness, made me more relaxed and more nervous at the same time. I then tiptoed back to our room, returned to bed, and saw you running to the cemetery. The wrought iron gates were locked, but you jumped over, ran past the closed empty chapels and the sleeping guards, past the dragon water tap, straight to the alley where, a few spots away from each other, Mother and V lie buried. The night was moonless, but the sky was clear, and the air was still hot. You just stood there and waited, as if knowing what was coming. The moment the breeze swooped in, raising the dried leaves of grass, fallen pine needles, the hairs on your skin, the apparitions began emerging from the tombstones—some resembling their portraits in marble, some looking much older, all standing still, but following vibrations of the air at the same time. Mother and V looked at you, I'm certain, and I saw you looking back. Could you tell by their otherworldly pallor how they died? Did they ask you anything at all? Everyone kept still. For a moment, I think I saw you floating, too. And then you ran back, sneaked into the apartment, got into the shower, and returned to bed, all wet. Where were you, I remember asking. Running, you said. You then ran your fingers over my crotch, and we did it quietly, and fast. Which I suppose you wouldn't want to write Amy about anyways. Oh, hon, where will all this take us?

∞

Amy, babe,

Four more days and we'll be on our way back. It's been a week already that we're in this house. (See the attachment—nice, right?) The kids spend most of their time with the nanny we hired and her children, and pretty much all of it in the water which, for a change, is warm and inviting. Seafood is all we eat, and Miloš and I practically live on the veranda, reading, staring at the massive mountains that overlook the bay, and stepping inside only to, well...you know. (A few times a day, if you can believe it.) It's a rare state of bliss, which I'm not going to spoil by writing too much about. The only (mis)adventure that I should mention was a boat trip, which we undertook so Miloš could show me the beach that he used to talk about so much—the one that *long time ago, before the tourists and the yachts* (remember?) was the most pristine cove on the Adriatic coast. The kids seemed to have too much fun with their new friends, so we hired our nanny's husband to take us there. As I was admiring the scenery (a few more pics attached), the two of them were discussing something in Serbo-Croatian, way beyond the reach of my comprehension. When we got there, a few boats were already tied to an abandoned marina, which was once touted as a great development opportunity for the area, something that would rake in big money, but whose owner took off one day and never came back. (Some say he's in prison, some that he defrauded a number of dangerous individuals and is now hiding in the Amazon delta.) A dilapidated shack with an open bar was also there, its name—*O Paraíso*, I believe—now almost completely illegible. Ridiculously enough, and true to Miloš's testimony, a good half of the beach was sliced up with these bizarre zig-zagging concrete pathways, covered in goat droppings and sprouting handfuls of corroded iron rods at regular intervals. The other people were enjoying themselves—after all, the beach is not really accessible from the land and still can provide some respite from the modern times. Miloš, however, didn't take it so well and, before we had a chance to take a dip, he asked our host to take us back to the safety of our veranda. And yes, David called, the very same day after dinner. I picked up, then passed the phone over to Miloš, who was curt and borderline unpleasant, apparently still recovering from our field trip. Oh, well. As we both know, there are side stories and after-stories to every story.

I find it difficult to leave this place, but also can't wait to see you and tell you everything that couldn't be written about.

Homesick in bikini,

K.

∞

And I'm homesick in the nude, content *and* restless, exhausted by your sterling contours that glow in the moonlight. In Nellie's words, *there's a problem with my soul*, and as you know, I don't even buy into the whole concept—or should I call it a *phenomenon*? Also, the fact that David called doesn't matter a bit. The veranda hours, on the other hand, do. So does the air from the bay that streams in through the windows and dries our skin. And the kids, shouting from the shallows, their voices echoing against the mountains. And us, eating grapes and watermelon on the Albion Street beach. And the skull-splitting heat of our bedroom in winter, which gives me nightmares but also makes your sweat glands emanate their best. So, hon, in light of a commonplace and somewhat sentimental observation that the time-place-memory continuum is constantly shrinking and corroding our brains, I wish your emails to Amy were longer. I wish our walks together were longer. I wish we remembered those sonnets. So I'm keeping these. I'm not deleting anything.

WHOLE LIFE

It was the time before the tourists and the yachts, before there was tap water and an asphalt road. The power wasn't on every day, either. In those days, the night would descend upon us unhindered, through the crowns of *zelenika* trees, absorbing and releasing the sounds on its way: the cicadas would calm down, the hum of the sea would grow louder, and not long afterward, the invisible people would start treading the pillows of dry leaves. Those must be ghosts, I'd proclaim, dead-certain, and my mother and father would agree. No, V would intervene: those are just hedgehogs. At night, when they walk on those leaves, hedgehogs sound just like people. We'd then spend some more time sitting on the porch and taking in the sounds, the cicadas' faint deliberations and the breaking of the waves, and then we'd retreat to our improvised beds on the dining room floor. V seems to be in good shape, my mother would proclaim, in her delicate whisper; thank goodness, my father would reply. I'd pretend to be asleep and they'd go on murmuring in the dark, although they must've known that I was sleuthing, that I was breathing like a child set on unearthing the unspoken. Before the flood of slumber would wash me away, V would appear from the only bedroom in the house—her hair undone, a gas lamp in her hand—and say c'mon, kids, you'd better go to sleep now. She'd then return to the same bed in which she was born, and in which her parents expired.

V would often tell the story of how she gave birth completely unassisted. No one was even there—at this point, she'd make a wrinkled vessel out of her elongated palms—to bring her as much as a glass of water. Only on every third or fourth occasion, her mustached father would appear—a knife in his hand, back from fishing, or forest, or shelter—right on time to sever the cord and deliver her from the bloodied, screaming coil. She seemed not to notice such inconsistencies; after all, she'd tell her stories only after her evening dose of anxiolytics was washed down with the obligatory few shots of grappa. And after the torment of birth and the curses that ensued, the bullets' whistles and the tying of the cord (and finally, after the sky-piercing cry of the infant, which, carried away, she'd try to imitate), V would ask that we each have one more glass. She'd then down hers in two short and focused movements, while I would use mine to soak the already grayed and solidified puff of cotton, and go on massaging her back. Press, my child, press harder, grappa is the cure for the diseased, she would keep repeating, and I'd keep rubbing as hard as I could, trying not to breathe in the vapors of alcohol, heavily spiced with odors of old age. Press right there, *moj sine*, that's where it's stuck, she'd squeeze through her teeth, as if sucking on a bitter candy, as if enjoying the itching pain she must've been in. About that moment, I'd begin to marvel at the redness the size of a child's palm, growing brighter at the exact spot where a splinter from a German grenade supposedly lay buried. Our sessions would end abruptly, cut short by my parents returning from their evening stroll, bringing in the scents of tobacco smoke and algae.

I was fifteen that summer, when Father took me to spend the entire school break with V. I guess it was still early; we really didn't have the time to talk it over. A week after the school was finished and after people stopped laying siege on our apartment, he said that I needed to pack. He also added that I'm big enough to understand some things, and that I ought to be at my bravest and at my most mature. Besides, he whispered, staring at an undefined spot behind my shoulder, I too need to get a grip on a few things, you know; you'll have a much better time staying with her for a while. When we arrived at V's place, Father just gave me a quick kiss on a cheek and hurried back to his car. Son, won't you at least have something to eat? she shouted from the porch, but Father just cast me the shortest of glances, muttered *be good to your baba*, and drove into the night.

Luckily, Mother died very fast, at the very end of the school year. I say luckily, because I knew that the end was approaching. A month before the "appendectomy" was done, I was spying more eagerly than ever on the whispers she and Father worked to conceal. The doctor was still convinced that it was just nothing, a twisted bile sac at worst, but she knew, and I knew too, that the words of the good doctor meant very little in this world. After a month, everything was over, and so was school. Everyone immediately rushed to the seaside, leaving me and my father alone, with an unoccupied seat at the table, on the couch, and in the car.

That summer, I used to have the ugliest of dreams. They would all invariably end with curtains of thick smoke, and a sensation of strong smell scrubbing at my nostrils. Although the smell was oddly familiar, it took me at least a week of waking up to it to figure it out. Once I did, still half-awake, I started expecting another sensation: the sound of a tin tray, clicking softly against the surface of the outdoor table. Oh, why do old people like coffee so much, I remember asking myself, and oh, why the hell do they get up so early? Still under my slumberous hangover, I'd fantasize appropriately: they loved coffee because they believed in the rejuvenating warmth of the *džezva* pot; or they were somehow finding solace in the sight of a cube of sugar, vanishing in silence in its hot, liquid abyss. As a natural consequence of such cogitations, I'd sometimes feel like getting up early, having the first cup of coffee of my life, and then writing a short poem about the impermanence of human existence and the rituals of the day—*Coffee, or Old Age* was its presumptive title.

Without an exception, however, my plans would be thwarted by M, who lived next door and always managed to show up before I had time to get my act together. She couldn't stop talking, stood a mere meter and a half tall, and had had a nickname of Big branded on her for longer than anyone could remember. While the two women were going through the newspapers and the village gossip—yes, my dear, oh, whaddo you say, oh, don't ask, I know, my sweetie—I'd be trying, without much success, to come up with some brilliant verses for my poem. Their chatter was hopelessly distracting, so the only thing I could succeed at was pretending to be asleep. It was sickening: in the entire village, there lived no one under the age of sixty; all in all, twelve stone houses with tiny, rectangular windows and blinds the color of pine needles. The only place where I was not surrounded by the old and the frail was the beach. As I said: it was the time before the tourists and the yachts. The beach could be reached only over the rocks and through a thorny shrub, and I was the only one in the entire village who could perform such a feat.

In the spring of forty-five, when Germans finally retreated, Big M was the first one to return. The village was not burnt down, but it was deserted and overgrown by creepers. The goats either had gone wild or had gone away. The first couple of days M spent in total darkness, in her house like a cave, because she was afraid to open the windows or light up the lamp. Soon afterward, the other villagers began to arrive. Among the last to return were V's parents, bringing with them a three-year-old child. We don't know if she's in this or in the other world, they'd say, if someone asked; she went off to the forest and never came back. She practically didn't breastfeed the poor thing; we barely managed to keep him alive.

Then another year and a half went by. Big M recalls that it was a Saturday when she looked up from her window and saw V coming down the steep goat path to the village. Her cheeks were all dried up and her hair was short, like in women who escaped soul asylums or internment camps. She burst into the yard like a smiling ghost, her arms spread toward her mother and child. The child screamed in terror and ran into the house.

Occasionally, my beach would be invaded by the uninvited, filthy visitors jumping out of their motor boats and ruining my day. Not only that I couldn't bathe naked with them around: that summer, I was also in a great need of solitude. Therefore, each time I'd hear the menacing patter of the little engine, I'd run off into the nearby bushes and squat down as low as I could. Hidden behind a barrier of thorns, I'd focus all of my mental powers on chasing the intruders away, on imprinting into their jell-o brains the true legend of a beast that lives somewhere around, sleeps under the pebbles, and feeds on human hearts. Each and every time, however, I had no choice but to capitulate, squatting away the time of their visit in my hideout, as nude as a baby, and as mad as a fiery and timid leprechaun. The visitors would waste their time on sunbathing and eating, on exchanging vulgar braggadocios for having discovered the only pristine beach on the Adriatic coast, and I'd end up asking myself what's taking the night so long, and where the hell are all those hedgehogs when you need them the most.

When she wasn't telling stories of her giving birth, V would recollect the events of March, nineteen-forty-one. One of those days, the war was going to come; at least that's what she kept hearing from R, who was my mythical grandfather and the fallen hero of the struggle against the uninvited. Shut up, you silly man, may cats bite your tongue off: I just got my job, and I'm not going back to the village—not even if I'm driven at the point of a gun. My heroic grandfather would then put his arms on V's shoulders, and say don't worry, I'll protect you no matter what, which she'd reenact by grabbing her own shoulders with her twig-like fingers, strong and half-petrified with arthritis. My fingers would also be firm in their position, gathered around the almost dry lump of cotton, which was about to expire its last breath of alcohol. The less alcohol there was, the stronger I pushed, asking myself for the thousandth time why the grenade splinters are so sensitive to pressure, and how come this one glows so red, through flesh and through the skin.

It would take another year and a half for son and mother to embrace. Father claims that to be his earliest memory. In contrast to V, he tells his stories always the same way: a boy approaches a tall, meager-looking woman bent over an ironing board—in those days, my son, you'd have to fill the iron with hot coal—and pulls at her skirt. The woman leans over to the boy and asks what it is that he wants; the boy puts his arms around her neck, and requests loud and clear: I want you to peel me an apple. Right away, my son, the woman replies. I imagine it happening in an early spring, and on a sunny day; I can hear the sea foaming the rocks, I can see it turning brilliant-blue. I imagine the room smelling of fruit and of freshly ironed linen.

They were all getting on my nerves, and terribly so; I wished they'd end up swallowed by the sea and eaten by the fish. All it takes is a little bit of focus, and I can recall the increasingly louder coughing of the little engine, and the ever brighter whiteness of the boat. Concealed behind a wall of shrub, I first take notice of a man in a striped shirt, jumping into the shallow water and pulling the boat onto the beach gravel. C'mon, Kitty, let's go, says a woman with a faux-straw hat, upon which Miss Kitty, no doubt their spoiled and boring daughter, descends from the vessel. It's late afternoon. I'm squatting silently in my prison of thorns. I hope they'll soon get enough of their fun; I hope that soon they'll pick up their stuff and leave.

I've been squatting in my thorny bush for over an hour. I can't make a move without revealing myself. The longer I wait, the more my response to the question, hey boy, tell us what the hell are you doing, all naked in those bushes, would look like an excuse for some nasty business. The three of them show no signs of giving up; they even brought a sun umbrella. The woman has just prostrated herself over a huge beach towel, decorated with a school of floating turtles. I was watching as she spread it at her feet in one swift move, and as the top part of her swimsuit slid down her hourglass waist, revealing a pair of melon-shaped tits, which were as thoroughly tanned as her big shoulders and her tight abdomen. She must be a swimmer, I remember thinking.

As she's throwing herself on the towel, the man—now stripped of his striped shirt—emerges out of the water, as if in a well-choreographed scene, and sits down by her side, on the warm and polished pebbles. Hey, Tomcat, are your hands dry, she purrs, and he's already on the task, wiping off his palms against a couple of helpless towel reptiles. Then he reaches for a bag adorned with a garland of oversized lilies, and takes out a plastic bottle with the picture of a bare-assed child. Gliding over the woman's muscular back, the bottle leaves a smooth line of sunscreen in its wake. The man starts rubbing in the lotion: slowly, with fortitude, and without passion. The woman makes no sound, aside from letting out an occasional moan, proclaiming that mmmm, here's so mmmm.

The man and the woman seem to be asleep now: she, half-wrapped in the umbrella's shadow; he, entirely exposed to the muted afternoon sun. All this time, Miss Kitty is in the water. Through the web of dusty vegetation and the shiny, jittery threads the sun bounces off the sea, she sometimes takes on a shape of nothing more than a dot, and sometimes the undisputable features of a female, with tar-black hair shining down her neck and covering her eyes. I wonder how much longer I will have to maintain my humiliating position. To kill time, I try to think of something, just anything, but to no avail.

She's sitting in the shallows, where I can see her better. She must be thirteen or fourteen, and has her mother's muscular back. Hey, Kitty, come over here, the topless woman calls out; let's have some peaches. Miss Kitty stands up and stretches her lanky body. She's wearing a white bikini with large, navy-blue polka dots. She approaches the man and the woman and lowers herself onto the towel. All three of them are now shielded by the umbrella's distorted shadow and gathered around a genuine picnic basket, one of those padded with neat checkered twill. More than ever, I feel like a complete and innocent victim of a cruel and inconsiderate invasion. Currents of strong, inarticulate rage start racing through my body. Only then do I realize that I'm having the most spectacular erection of my life.

All of a sudden, I'm becoming painfully aware that I'm naked and sore from an entire hour and a half of squatting. My enormous penis occasionally touches the warm and desiccated earth. With a sound no louder than a gasp of astonishment would make, a well-gnawed peach seed lands right next to its hugely augmented head. A couple of filaments of the peach flesh are still clinging to the seed, attracting rust-colored particles from the ground. The next seed lands in my lap.

Just keep still, I say to myself; this is hardly your first hiding, you know you're invisible. Then I see her standing up, hear her saying I gotta pee, and count the ten or so steps she makes toward the bushes. Trying not to catch her gaze, I focus on the patch of earth between my feet, where a sentry unit of red ants hurries busily toward the moist remnants of peach flesh. Miss Kitty finds her way through the thicket rather quickly, and comes to a halt only a few meters away from my hideout. She pulls down her bikini bottom and rolls down into a firm squat. A gold-yellow liquid bursts out from between her thighs, hitting the ground audibly, and starts running down toward her toes. In order not to wet herself, she rotates by a quarter of a circle; now we're face to face, and both wearing no panties.

I don't know what happens first: do I avert my gaze from hers, or take notice that she has far more pubic hair than I do? I don't know whether my mouth is open, and if my face gives away the thrilling fear I'm awash with. I don't know what I should do, once I become aware of her bright-green eyes and the puffed-up lips, crossed by the line of her index finger. I don't know what to do, except to return her sign of silence, and make sure that I don't drop my pitiful bundle of clothes. My erratic eyes are taking in her face, her breasts, and the spread of her legs, still pouring out a shy little stream. I see three thin curving traces of urine, making their way toward me. And that's pretty much all I remember from our encounter. I still can somewhat recall the industrious platoon of ants, making their path to the seed of the peach, only to be swept away by the flood that smells of fecundity and sin, and how I think that I'm going to blow into pieces.

What are you doing, you asshole, you little motherfucker: those are the words carried by a hoarse barking voice, words I fail to register until she jumps up, pulling up her pants and letting out a silent scream. A thick, purple head is looming over mine, from above the walls of once-impenetrable bushes. Daddy, don't, I hear her saying as she retreats a step, but he's already pushing through the thorns, shoving them left and right with the beach towel, whose one end is tied in a knot that looks like a cubist turtle sculpture. I'm sorry, please, I didn't, I babble in vain, as I take the hit of the towel ball straight into my face. My nose begins to bleed. I drop my clothes and begin to run.

I don't know for how long I was running through the bushes, with hands in front of my eyes. I don't know if or for how long her raging father was breathing down my neck. Sometimes I had a feeling that he was but a step away, and that the knot, now overgrown with spikes of all sizes, kept catching up with my back and the back of my head. I didn't turn even once. I ran and ran, until I tripped over a stone or some root and hit the ground with the full force of my battered body. Around me there was no one and nothing, except for a razor-sharp labyrinth of leaves. My wounds had not yet started to burn, but I was cut all over, and covered with blood like a newborn. Fighting the gasps, I remained on the ground as long as I could, trying to keep low my heavy, swollen head. Slowly, it was becoming clear that I didn't know where I was. The colors were burning out; the cicadas were winding down their song; I thought I could hear an intermittent sound of a small boat engine. It was late, the night was falling.

In my dream, I first saw Grandpa R, who did not say a word. Instead, he opened the skies like a curtain and pointed at V, who was breastfeeding an infant with a head of a vampire bat. Then a gigantic Messerschmitt flew over, followed by the sounds of metallic thunder and *L'Internationale*, and a machine gun fired, and grandpa fell on the ground, cut in pieces. V stepped forth, took over the rims of the sky-curtain from his dead fingers, and sewed them together in one move. Then she turned away from me and disappeared into a darkness that was descending with an unnatural speed, but not before I could spot a piece of white-hot metal glowing between her shoulder blades. Then out of the darkness my mother emerged, with her porcelain skin and her belly sliced wide open. She was grinning widely, and gesturing that everything was fine, and that her abdominal cave, with its sheen of nacre, was now depleted of every single organ. She moved toward me and took me in a strong, motherly embrace. The entire universe began to shake uncontrollably.

Wake up, son, wake up, says the voice behind the off-yellow light. Big M takes me under the arm and lifts me up with an unexpected strength. Wha' happened, you little fool? Tha' woman's dead-worried, you know. Which woman, I remember thinking. I have no idea where I am: I only know that it's night, that I'm naked, and that my whole body is covered with bruises and wounds. All I see is an uneven dance of two weak electric torches; all I can hear are voices of two women, calling out to each other. Finally, V and Big M drag me to the house and lay me on a bed. V tries to run her fingers through my crown of thorns; Big M brings me a glass of cold milk. V then fills her palms with grappa. Grappa is the cure for the diseased, I need to disinfect you, *kućo moja*, she keeps saying as she runs her hands up and down my body, blowing into my countless burning wounds, and as I begin to cry, as if giving birth.

A couple of evenings later, Father showed up, looking twenty years older. My wounds were healing well and were barely visible in the dark; I couldn't, didn't want to tell him a thing. We sat down together, he and I, on the wooden bench in front of the house. Above our heads, through the crowns of *zelenika* trees, a glowing night was descending. I thought that it would never end, and that I'd stay awake forever. Do you know how far the light travels in one year? I know, I said. We kept sitting like that, staring at the stars, I don't know for how long. Then the leaves started to rustle, as if trodden over by invisible people. So there they are, father said. C'mon now, we'd better go to sleep.

NOTES

According to Leonardo da Vinci, sfumato is a painting technique in which the object is presented "without lines or edges, as if seen through smoke or out of focus"—in other words, the way we often think of memories.

In the omnibus story "Table of Discontents," the segment "Nuages" was titled after the Django Reinhardt's jazz standard; better said, after the sublime version from the album The Big 3 (Milt Jackson, vibraphone; Joe Pass, guitar; Ray Brown, bass; Pablo Records, 1976). The writing of "Rearrangements" was fueled by incessant listening to Dvořák's Concerto for Cello in B-minor, mostly the version recorded around 1970 by Mstislav Rostropovich and the Berlin Philarmonic Orchestra (conductor Herbert von Karajan; Deutsche Gramophon), as well as by J. S. Bach's Cello Suites

(Rostropovich again), recorded in March 1991 in the cathedral of Vézelay, France. The other stories were mainly written while listening to J. S. Bach's Goldberg Variations, as interpreted by Simone Dinnerstein (2007), Glenn Gould (1955 and 1981), and Jeremy Denk (2013).

The stories "American Sfumato," "Rattus," and "Re: Nellie McKay Sonnets" were inspired, respectively, by the Todd Haynes' Bob Dylan pseudo-biopic *I'm Not There*, Danilo Kiš's novel *The Hourglass*, and the music and lyrics of Nellie McKay.

Also, let there be known that I got the idea of planting an anecdote about Danilo Kiš surrounded by a cohort of female fans (fully invented, of course) into a story that also features Jean-Paul Belmondo *before* I came across the Rhoda Koenig report from the 1986 PEN conference in New York ("At play in the fields of the word: Alienation, imagination, feminism, and foolishness at PEN", *New York Magazine*, February 3, 1986), which relates the following:

"According to opinions from both sexes, the best-looking delegate was the happy, approachable Vargas Llosa ('Isn't he *unbearably* handsome!' cried a woman in front of me at one panel), but the most appealing was Danilo Kiš, variously referred to as 'that charismatic Yugoslav' and 'the literary Jean-Paul Belmondo.' Talk about not being able to judge a writer by his book cover—Kiš is the author of *A Tomb for Boris Davidovich*, an excellent but horribly grim novel that the jacket blurb describes as a 'fictionalized account of the self-destruction of [the] Comintern.' At the library party, I discovered a slender, smiling man with bushy hair leaning against a column and, when I conveyed my admiration, was told I was *'adorable et charmant'* (Kiš's English is minimal) and got my hand kissed, or, rather, inhaled. Later, I returned to his corner to find him draped with pretty girls. 'You seem to have many ladies,' I remarked in French. *'Oui,'* he sighed, the smoke from his Gauloise describing a trajectory of brooding resignation, *'J'ai toujours beaucoup de femmes. Ça marche très bien au commencement.'"*

Ars gratia artis, but in moderation.

ACKNOWLEDGMENTS

This book was written in parallel in English and Serbo-Croatian, mostly while commuting. Therefore, I am first and foremost grateful to the employees of Chicago Transit Authority, particularly those in charge of the Purple Line, for the relatively reliable timetable and the mostly clean train cars. I'm also grateful to Amy Davis of WritersWorkSpace in Chicago, where the finishing touches were done.

In their English incarnations, a few stories from this book appeared in US literary journals, either as originals (Night Swim, *Kenyon Review*, 2014; Rearrangements, *Rivet Journal*, 2017) or as (self)translated pieces (Whole Life, *Kenyon Review Online*, 2011; Mannheim, *Prism Review*, 2015).

My decision to write stories was based on the belief—a naïve one, as it would turn out—that that would require less effort than writing a novel, and because once, long time ago, Svetlana Slapšak, a classicist, writer, editor, and friend, decided to give me a chance, publishing a few of my early works in *ProFemina*, a (the) Serbian feminist journal of the 1990s. I remain eternally in debt for that early encouragement and for the many hours of conversation and correspondence, which count among my most exciting intellectual adventures.

The nebula of ideas that preceded the writing of this book coalesced into sfumato completely by surprise, one winter night in 2009, in a high rise by Chicago's Belmont Harbor, in between the cinnamon-spiced pork roast and espresso, catalyzed by an offhand remark about the importance of longing in everyday life. The remark's author was my sage friend Ruth Blatt, who also took on the responsibility of critically reading every story in the book whose creation she sparked. I remain thankful for the friendship, the wisdom, the many meals together.

Svetlana Vuković, a Serbian journalist, invested many hours in reading everything I was sending her, both in English and Serbo-Croatian, and helped me a great deal in understanding the characters I was creating. In addition, the great personal courage of her and her colleague Svetlana Lukić during the civil war in former Yugoslavia was an inspiration to write "Rearrangements," which features their brief cameo. Marija Backović and Miloš Ćirić were also very astute, very diligent readers.

Nicole Aragi, Katherine Fausset, Aleksandar Hemon, Petar Janković, Maja Milićević, Brigid Pasulka, and Dunja Vukojičić were the first who read the manuscript from the beginning to the end and encouraged me in thinking that the effort wasn't entirely misplaced. I'm also indebted to Millie Bahn, Eula Biss, Carol Brown, Joshua Corey, Judith DeWoskin, Rachel DeWoskin, Zayd Dohrn, Aleksandar Duravcevic, Nikola Duravcevic, Ivan Jovanović, Milica Jovanović, Autumn Kelly, Michael Leslie Miller, Nami Mun, Margaret A. Park, Dragan Prelević, Aleksandra Rekar, Charles Simic, Lada Stevanović, Marija Tešić-Schnell, Jess Thoene, and Yuan-Qing Yu for their friendship, knowledge, and attention to detail.

I owe it to the editorial brilliance and vision of Jerry Brennan, the heart, mind, and hawk eye behind Tortoise Books, that this tortoise of a book made it across the finish line.

Finally, as slim as this book is, I couldn't finish it without Ivana, Ivan, and Filip. I hope they'll find it in their hearts to forgive me.

ABOUT THE BOOK

American Sfumato consists of nine mesmerizing stories, each designed to function independently and form a unit with the rest. The action is set in several present-time locales (Chicago, the Balkans, New Orleans, Germany, Brazil), and the narrative revolves around a protagonist who's caught up in attempts to reassemble the fragments that constitute his life. By day, he's a neurobiologist who researches learning and memory, which then informs his acts of nighttime self-examination.

The Serbo-Croatian version was published in Montenegro and Serbia in 2015, and a Slovenian translation was released in 2016. In 2016, *American Sfumato* was nominated for the Meša Selimović Prize, the most prestigious award for a novel published in Bosnia, Croatia, Montenegro, or Serbia, and in 2017, it was shortlisted as a Montenegrin entry for the European Union Prize for Literature.

ABOUT TORTOISE BOOKS

Slow and steady wins in the end, even in publishing. Tortoise Books is dedicated to finding and promoting quality authors who haven't yet found a niche in the marketplace—writers producing memorable and engaging works that will stand the test of time.

Learn more at www.tortoisebooks.com, find us on Facebook, or follow us on Twitter @TortoiseBooks.